The Tenant

A Novella

Odella Howe

Fiddleback Press

Copyright © 2026 by Odella Howe

All rights reserved.

No portion of this book may be reproduced in any form without written permission from the publisher or author, except as permitted by U.S. copyright law, nor used to train AI technology.

This is a work of fiction. Names, characters, businesses, places, events, and incidents are either products of the author's imagination or used in a fictitious manner. Any resemblance to actual persons, living or dead, or actual events is purely coincidental.

Contents

Quote Page	1
1. Chapter 1	3
2. Chapter 2	11
3. Chapter 3	20
4. Chapter 4	29
5. Chapter 5	38
6. Chapter 6	47
7. Chapter 7	54
8. Chapter 8	65
9. Chapter 9	72
10. Chapter 10	82
11. Chapter 11	90
12. Chapter 12	99
13. Chapter 13	107
14. Chapter 14	113
15. Chapter 15	118
16. Chapter 16	122

Acknowledgments	126
Could You Do Me A Favor?	128
About The Author	129
Also By Odella Howe	130

If a man harbors any sort of fear, it percolates through all his thinking, damages his personality, makes him landlord to a ghost.
Henry Ward Beecher

Chapter One

Pain begets pain, a fact Marvin had learned many times over as a landlord. This time, the trouble was at the Riverbrook apartments.

The voice of the complex's on-site manager rose to hysteria. "Please, Mr. Hoeff, the situation here is a mess. I insist you come at once."

Marvin heaved a sigh, further irritated by Abhi's obligate politeness. He drummed his fingers, narrowing his eyes at the phone on his desk as though it were personally responsible for his irritation.

"As soon as possible, please, sir. I am out of my depth here," Abhi continued.

Marvin hunched over his desk, rubbing his temples. "Fine. I'll be there"—Marvin checked his watch that read 8:32 AM—"within an hour or so." He hung up, cutting short Abhi's response.

An hour would leave him time to grab a McMuffin and a coffee before heading to the Riverbrook complex to deal with the situation. If he ran a bit late, so be it.

As Marvin shut his laptop, stood from his chair, and collected his wallet and keys, he considered once again how overrated the job of a landlord was. No one recognized how he made space for people who couldn't help themselves.

People. Rats, more like it. Vermin, always seeking special considerations, lowered payments, returned deposits, better appliances than he himself had, and, in general, seemed to delight in making his life as difficult as possible.

Ingrates. If they understood half the work he did, they would worship at his feet. Repairs? On him. Pest control? Him too. Everything on him, always.

Sure, there was decent money to be made, but never enough credit for what he put in. Especially on days like today and the situation with Colette.

Colette.

He never looked forward to being on site at his properties. Even under the best of circumstances, he was loath to come face-to-face with his tenants. If they weren't trying to, say, pull one over on him for an unregistered, un-deposited-for mongrel of a dog, they always had one complaint or another.

I saw a roach in my kitchen.

My toilet is too low. Can it be replaced?

My upstairs neighbor keeps blasting music at two in the morning. Can you ask her to stop?

I dropped something in the garbage disposal. Fish it out for me, won't you?

As though Marvin himself were the goddamn maintenance manager for the building instead of that good-for-nothing, pink-haired Benny, who was probably stoned out of his mind again instead of doing his job. Benny was just lucky he'd never asked Marvin for a raise—it was the only reason he still had a job.

Would the tenants dare complain to him today, he wondered, or might they have some kind of deference for his situation and save it for another day? Marvin could only hope so. He had enough bullshit to deal with.

Colette.

Marvin glowered, mentally cursing her name. Where her problems had ended, his had only begun. He stepped outside into a July morning nearing ninety degrees. The oppressive heat didn't improve his mood. At least this particular tenant couldn't bother him anymore. Colette Finch was no longer his problem. Yet, that wasn't really true. Marvin wasn't exactly free of her—or her remains, anyway. This was far from the typical move-out.

The situation here is a mess.

It sure fucking was, Abhi. It sure fucking was. And Marvin refused to deal with any of it before he'd eaten.

"Jesus Christ."

Marvin stood in the doorway of the flooded bathroom regretting his breakfast muffin. The tub brimmed with red-tinged water. Several pairs of boot prints, presumably from the emergency responders, tracked the bloody mess all the way through the apartment to the front door.

"What the fuck," he breathed.

The razor with which Colette had ended her life had been sloshed onto the floor, left to rust. The baseboards in the bathroom were drenched in a mixture of body fluids and bathwater.

On the counter, Colette's makeup was still scattered about. The sink was crusted with days' worth of toothpaste spittle. The mirror was smudged and spotted all over. It wasn't just the blood; this tenant had been a slob in life too.

"I am sorry you must see this bad situation," said Abhi tentatively. "But now you understand why I called you."

Marvin shook his head. "Bad doesn't begin to cover it. Do you have any idea what this will cost?" He glared into Abhi's dark eyes, wondering whether he would dare attempt an answer. When he didn't, Marvin elaborated. "It's not just about the vacancy. She didn't exactly give us the customary thirty-day notice, did she? Look at all this. Water damage? Biohazard cleaning? Her deposit won't cover half of this."

As he looked over the soaked floor, his pulse began to throb in his ears. "Goddamn it, this water probably soaked all the way through to the subfloor." He raised an eyebrow at Abhi. "The downstairs apartment — is it affected?"

Abhi nodded soberly. "They say they will be staying in a hotel for a while. Until this is cleaned."

"How nice for them," drolled Marvin.

Abhi's brow furrowed.

Marvin paid little mind, consumed as he was with his tirade. "So what's next? This place can't be turned over anytime soon. What a fucking mess. This is going to cost a damn *fortune*."

Abhi remained silent, which rankled Marvin. Couldn't he get a little sympathy here? As soon as Abhi spoke, however, Marvin missed the silence.

"Surely your other properties may sustain you, sir. This complex alone has 108 units."

Marvin balked. "That's not their *job*. How is that fair? Everyone pays their own way." Without waiting for a response, Marvin asked the next question on his mind. "Guessing she lives alone, so no husband?"

Abhi paused, an unreadable expression on his face. "No, sir."

"Boyfriend?"

Another shake of the head.

There has to be someone, thought Marvin. "Who's her emergency contact?"

"Her father," said Abhi tentatively, gesturing to the folder in his arms, which Marvin hadn't noticed. Finally, a break.

"Looks like he's on the hook." Marvin made to grab for the folder, but Abhi moved it out of reach.

Marvin glared at him. Abhi stared back.

"Mister Hoeff." The tone was one of reproach, like a mother scolding a schoolboy. His accent strained under his incredulity, stretching his words into something more like *Meester Hoof*. This only annoyed Marvin more.

"*What?*" he snapped.

"This . . ." Abhi lowered his voice. "Do you understand what has happened here, sir? This is truly a great tragedy."

Shaking his head, Marvin scoffed. "Sure, I understand. Weirdo couldn't hack it, offed herself, and left everyone else to pick up the mess. Selfish, that's what I say."

Abhi stared at him silently.

"*What.*" A dare, not a question. Marvin had no time for games, not with the monumental task ahead of him. He could practically feel his bank account bleeding. "I'm sorry, but this is not my problem."

"You . . ." Abhi shook his head. "Sir, you—you are monstrous."

A vein throbbed in Marvin's temple. He glowered at Abhi, raising his arms to indicate the surrounding apartment. "This is the job, Abhi. If you can't do it, find another."

Abhi's dark eyes glanced toward the bathtub and back to Marvin. "You must try to find within your heart some respect for the dead."

"Not like she respected anyone else," scoffed Marvin.

Abhi tensed and, after a moment's pause, said, "Goodbye, sir. I wish you well." Marvin had expected a slammed door as he left, but Abhi shut it gently.

Marvin looked after him for a moment, then turned to assess the scene once more.

No one understands me, he thought morosely.

Over the next few hours, Marvin paced the sloshy apartment as he made several furious phone calls to Colorado Disaster Cleanup to arrange the cleaning of the apartment, the Greenville police to gain access to the official police report, the Greenville fire department to complain about their treatment of his property, the Greenville County morgue to ask after a death certificate for Colette, which seemed a useful thing for any legal situations forthcoming, the main city of Greenville to suggest the mayor implement landlord protections for such situations as tenant suicide, and anyone and everything remotely connected to the Colette Situation, as he soon thought of it. He wouldn't stop until he saw some kind of justice.

Having finally worn himself down, he pulled out a chair and sat at Colette's wobbly folding table, surveying the rest of the apartment. On the built-in shelves of the apartment were an assortment of tacky souvenir snow globes, statues of various birds, and succulents in kitschy planters. *Nothing worth selling here*, he thought.

Nothing but cat-less crazy cat lady tchotchkes and the cheapest furniture possible.

Waste. Just a goddamn waste of time and money. *His* time and money.

It was six o'clock by the time his calls were finished. Not that Marvin had finished airing his grievances, but everyone who might field them had closed for the day. He might have accomplished more had he not been interrupted by phone calls from other property managers, other tenants who had somehow found his number, or the occasional tenant stopping by to offer condolences. Not for his financial situation, of course, but for *poor Colette.*

No sympathy for him. Typical.

"Her problems are over," he would remind them before getting back on track with his phone calls.

The final gut punch was realizing that in all the calls he had made, he had neglected to call Colette's father regarding his financial responsibility in the matter. Marvin opened the folder on the table and pulled out Colette's lease agreement. Under the heading *Emergency Contact*, he found what he was looking for: *David Finch, Father*, written in Colette's untidy scrawl, followed by the man's phone number marked *(cell).*

Marvin dialed the number, laid the phone on the table, and set it to speaker.

Ring. Ring. Ring.

"Hello, you have reached the voicemail b—"

Marvin punched END CALL, in too foul a mood to leave a proper message. It would be a job for tomorrow after all.

When his stomach growled, Marvin realized he hadn't eaten since breakfast. Fortunately, the Green Dragon would be happy to serve him dinner on the way home.

As he locked up, Marvin consoled himself, thinking of all the needed repairs in the unit as a potential blessing in disguise. The biohazard-necessitated renovation could be upsold as upgraded, modernized. And—did he dare dream?—if insurance paid for the upgrades, the apartment could certainly be rented for several hundred more a month. Any monetary recompense received from the father could be used to update other units. Depending on how he played it, he might use the funds to invest in another property.

Marvin smiled. Maybe that would make all this bullshit worth it. Even so, it would be a long road before any kind of payoff.

"Thanks, Colette. Thank you for everything," drawled Marvin as he shut the door on the mess, wishing like hell to leave it all behind, but knowing in his heart he would return bright and early the next day.

Chapter Two

Marvin returned home bearing his usual from the Green Dragon, the Kung Pao combo with a Coke. Its plastic wrapping read THANK YOU FOR YOUR PATRONAGE and was topped with the customary fortune cookie. By the time he pulled into the driveway, it was well past dark, which made him grumpy. Managing properties into the evening was not what he'd signed up for. Marvin so disliked being the face of the company, he had hired people like Abhi to do it for him.

He entered the kitchen and sat at the island, his forlorn dining table serving more as a class symbol than a functional piece. With his phone in one hand and a fork in the other, Marvin scrolled Facebook but stopped upon reaching a post advertising a GoFundMe for someone named Nathaniel. Marvin narrowed his eyes at the post—it was a schmaltzy thing, entitled *Help This Angel On Earth Find A Home.*

His thumb hovered over the link before he finally gave in to the masochistic urge to read it. It was the same old nonsense about how selfless this Nathaniel was, and how he deserved a little help like the help he had given others, yadda yadda yadda.

Marvin exited the page, left a laughing emoji on the post, then put his phone down.

Why such things were allowed, he wasn't sure. Panhandling was illegal, being the eyesore it was. So why should his vision be assaulted by the digital version? He had no money to spare, especially after a day of huge losses like he had faced today.

Maybe if this Nathaniel had been better at managing his own business, he wouldn't be sleeping in a garbage bag.

With that thought, Marvin finished off the Kung Pao chicken and chicken fried rice and washed it down with the last of his Coke. He cracked open his fortune cookie and settled in to read the future within—just for fun. It read:

An exciting opportunity lies ahead of you.

19   9   11   23   25   13

Marvin scoffed. "Bullshit."

Unless it was talking about the opportunity to clean up that awful apartment, the cookie was definitely full of shit.

He tossed the slip into the THANK YOU FOR YOUR PATRONAGE bag, now destined for the trash, ate the bland, somewhat stale cookie, then departed to rest and relax from his stressful day. The next day was bound to be full of just as much bullshit as the last. Such was guaranteed, since he would have the displeasure of calling David Finch to collect on the debt which his daughter had so callously left behind. If this Mr. Finch was wise, he would pay up without Marvin having to resort to more radical measures. No one liked being taken to court.

Marvin clomped up the stairs to his bedroom, where he looked forward to taking a shower to wash away the sour, unpleasant smell of the apartment. Why had he stayed so long? After he brushed his teeth, he would stream something stupid before heading to bed. He would surely sleep peacefully, carrying as great a burden of guilt as a two-year-old might after screaming for a cookie—which is to say, none.

If Marvin had thought to look, however, he might have seen the pair of baleful eyes from the shadows, watching his ascent. He might have understood the primal chill up his spine and roiling of his stomach as more than Green Dragon-induced indigestion.

Those primitive alarm bells had good reason to ring. Something had followed him home.

Marvin cast a look downstairs before shaking his head and turning the corner. With the fever-like chill rising within him, he grew more irritable. *Just what I need, getting sick.*

He tried to recall what his mother might have done. Maybe a bath, one with plenty of Epsom salt. Or was it baking soda? Vinegar?

The allure of the idea was extinguished by the recollection of Colette's death. Marvin shuddered, his steps faltering. No, a bath would decidedly not be nice. A bath might never be nice again.

A shower would do.

He continued up the stairs. *A nice, hot shower*, he thought as a whiff of sourness assaulted his nostrils once more. He would run it until the water ran out, if that's what it took to rid himself of the smell which permeated his clothes, one which did not improve by being overlaid with the scent of Kung Pao.

His stomach turned. Was it indigestion getting to him? He *had* eaten rather quickly. Or maybe it was food poisoning. Yes, food poisoning would be just his luck after his miserable day. On the bright side, he could at least complain his way into a refund for his meal. If not, he'd get them shut down. Plenty of other Chinese restaurants existed in the area. The Green Dragon was convenient, sure, but Marvin had no particular loyalty to it.

His room was dark and cool, just the way he liked it. He passed through and entered the bathroom, lighting it with the dimmer of the two light fixtures and turning on the fan. Beneath the sink was an assortment of grocery bags. Marvin stripped off his clothing and put them in one bag, tying it off to deal with another day. The Foxglove complex had coin-operated machines. If Marvin used those, he could reduce the risk of the smell getting into his personal machine. He wouldn't even need to pay: once he unscrewed the coin box, he could recycle some of the quarters and be good to go.

He looked over the clothes critically for a moment, wondering if he might not just throw them away.

Turning his attention to the shower, he turned the water tap all the way to the red. When it nearly scalded his hand, Marvin turned it down a bit. That cold chill came again, sending a shiver up Marvin's spine.

It had better not be food poisoning, he thought miserably as he stepped into the shower and shut the door behind him. The steady stream of hot water drenched his body and mollified his misery almost at once. He let out a satisfied groan as the water beat on his tense muscles.

Marvin rubbed shampoo between his hands and massaged his scalp, then rinsed, closing his eyes against the spray. A fear long buried since childhood leaped to his mind. *What if there's a face right there, inches from my own, when I open my eyes?* This imagined terror was replaced by the certainty that there was, in fact, someone there.

His eyes flashed open, but of course there was nothing.

Marvin swallowed hard, shaking his head at his own absurdity. *It's just because of the damn apartment. Fucking Colette offing herself. The whole mess is fucking with me.*

Heart rate returning to normal, Marvin finished rinsing his hair, then lathered a washcloth and scrubbed the rest of his body. He rubbed his skin raw, grating his skin with the vigor of one refinishing an antique. The sooner and more thoroughly he washed it all away, the better.

Upon turning off the water, Marvin reconsidered his plans for the night. Maybe television was a bad idea. What he really needed was a good night's sleep. More calls would have to be made the next day—not just to Mr. Finch, but to Marvin's lawyer too. Jamie would probably be willing to take the case, but after Abhi's reaction, Marvin wondered whether he would have to find someone seedier.

If such a thing were possible, thought Marvin with a chuckle.

As he stepped out of the shower, he pondered the case. When one got past sentimentality and respect for the dead, there was a genuine claim to be made. The months left on the lease would remain unpaid on an apartment which couldn't be occupied until the requisite biohazard cleaning was done. Marvin was sure the cost would be astronomical. That didn't factor in the intangibles: his own pain, trauma, and suffering of being at the scene.

He could tack on that of his employees, too. Marvin considered the way Abhi had stormed out of the apartment earlier. Might his reaction be different if he were able to get a little cash for the trouble?

Marvin grinned. *Most likely*, he thought, then said in a soft, sing-songy voice, "Money makes the world go round."

His face fell as another flush of cold washed over him, as did a bizarre impulse to cover himself, as if someone was watching.

Marvin turned. Had he heard . . . a *giggle*?

He stiffened, listening for a moment. *No*, he thought, drying the water from his body. No, it was the stress making him lose his goddamn mind.

But it *had* sounded like a giggle, and its echo within his mind enticed him to dress as quickly as possible.

As he pulled on his socks, he was sure it was time to hit the sack. No Netflix tonight. And he would turn off the air conditioner. It must be set too strong for him to be this cold when it was still at least eighty degrees outside.

Marvin's concern for his mental well-being deepened as he continued to prepare for bed. He was sure he caught glimpses of something out of the corner of his eye as he brushed his teeth. The feeling became so strong he was reluctant to look in the mirror.

"It's just the stress," he repeated like a mantra. "Just the stress. Nothing a good night's sleep can't fix."

He proceeded to bed looking directly at the floor, and closed his eyes as he settled in. He threw the blanket over his head and opened the app on his phone to turn down the air. He shivered while he waited for his ambient body heat to warm the space under the covers. He was sure he must be getting sick, feeling this cold.

If it was illness that was getting to him, Marvin would find no relief in sleep. To say he was unfamiliar with insomnia would be an understatement, prone as he was to falling asleep the moment his head hit the pillow. On this particular evening, however, it was like someone had left a light on in some portion of his brain. There was something niggling at him, like he was somehow exposed.

"What the fuck," he breathed, rolling to his back. What was his problem tonight? He stared at the ceiling.

A fetid smell rose to Marvin's awareness, and he groaned. How could he still stink? He had scrubbed in the shower with just less force than was needed to skin himself alive. How he still smelled of rotten eggs at low tide, Marvin wasn't sure.

He rolled to his other side in a huff. This terrible day simply refused to end.

While Marvin debated the utility of Febreze as bubble bath, he was annoyed to find a crawling sensation on the sole of his foot. He flinched, then reached to scratch at the irritation.

He paused. Was it. . . *wet*?

Just as Marvin was puzzling out this development, the same sensation manifested on his other foot. Marvin frowned, pulling both feet toward himself. *What the fuck?* Curled in the fetal position, he chanced a look toward the end of the bed.

What he saw made his heart leap into his throat, and he bolted upright.

Red, bright, gleaming eyes floated at the foot of his bed.

"What the *fuck*," said Marvin, out loud this time.

The red eyes rose steadily, revealing their owner. It was a ghastly white face, eyes ringed by dripping mascara. The creature giggled with its red-lipped grin. The sound sent Marvin's testicles hurtling toward his diaphragm. It was the same giggle he'd heard in the bathroom. He was sure of it.

"What the *fuck*," he said once more, unable to assemble his thoughts into more pertinent verbal questions like *who are you, what are you, why are you here,* or *can you please not hurt me.*

"*Hi*, Marvin." The visitor spoke with a childlike cadence, a determined seeker delighted to find the elusive hider. This incongruity, far from putting Marvin at ease, unraveled him. He began to shake.

When the creature used one hand to toss a sheet of long, dark hair over its shoulder, Marvin noticed something.

The hand was bloody, wrist sliced open wide. Its hair was wet, as if freshly bathed.

Marvin stared, awe-struck. It couldn't be. That was impossible. And yet, though he had never seen her in life, there was no doubt who stood at the foot of his bed.

"Colette?" Marvin squeaked.

She giggled again, bloody hand held coquettishly over her red lips. "Why, Marvin, I didn't realize you knew my name."

Marvin gazed at her, momentarily dumbstruck. He said, quite stupidly, "You're dead."

She nodded, an eyebrow raised. "Uh-huh."

Marvin paused, uncharacteristically without words. She watched him like a tiger would a wild boar. He gathered himself enough to repeat, "You're *dead*."

"Yes, darling. So noted."

"But . . ." He cleared his throat. "But that means you can't be here," said Marvin with a matter-of-factness that was perhaps intended to soothe himself. "*You can't be here*. This isn't real. I'm dreaming or hallucinating or going out of my goddamn mind."

But the thought went no further, interrupted by the rapid draining of amusement from the Colette-creature's face. Her eyes darkened. With unbelievable speed, she appeared directly above Marvin. Her mouth yawned wide, but her scream erupted within Marvin's own head, not from her mouth. He pressed his back against his mattress, looking into reddened eyes. She breathed like a rabid animal, her exhalations rancid in his face. Try as he might, Marvin was unable to get far enough away from Colette to avoid her undead hand as it slapped him hard across his face.

"This is as real as it fucking gets, *sweetheart*," said Colette.

Marvin, placing a hand upon his now-moist and foul-smelling cheek, was sure that he was, indeed, wide awake—and desperately wished he wasn't.

Chapter Three

"You're not dreaming, Marvin, and you can't get away from me. I'm here to teach you a lesson, and you're not going anywhere until I'm done." Colette spoke inches from his face, her pale blue eyes bloodshot and filled with rage.

Marvin squirmed, wiggling out from Colette's grasp. He fell off the bed in his desperation to be free, then looked back to take in the full sight of the apparition. She now sat on the edge of his bed, her dark hair mostly behind her back aside from what was plastered against her face. She wore a sundress covered with incongruously cheery sunflowers and forget-me-nots. These flowers might have been brighter before they had been tinged with bloody water, the same macabre dye which had turned what must have been white or yellow backing fabric a rusty orange color. Her legs were pale and bloodless, her feet bare. She wore a black cuff around one ankle, a detail which passed unexamined in the overwhelm of the rest.

"Fuck that," said Marvin, his voice quaking more than he would have preferred to admit. "This has to be a dream."

He made for the hallway. Marvin saw motion overhead momentarily and lost his footing at the sight, stumbling to the floor. Colette crawled across the ceiling like an oversized spider, coming to a stop within the doorway. She hung upside down, blocking his path. When she saw the way Marvin was rooted to the spot, she grinned. Marvin let out a gasp, covering his mouth.

"This isn't real, this isn't real, this isn't real," he repeated softly, but he couldn't tear his eyes away from the creature in the doorway.

Like a chicken, her head remained fixed in place as she crawled limb-over-limb to stand upon the carpet in the doorway, her gaze fixed on his the entire time.

This can't be real, Marvin thought, dropping his head as he squeezed his eyes shut. Maybe by the time he opened them, the apparition would be gone.

This vain hope evaporated as he heard squelchy footsteps coming in his direction.

I'm going to have a heart attack, thought Marvin. *I'm going to die. She's going to kill me.*

"You aren't getting it," she said. "I'm very real."

Reluctantly, Marvin looked up at the figure towering over him. If this wasn't a dream, if he wasn't yet out of his mind, he was sure to end up that way soon. "But you're dead."

"Naturally."

"This can't be fucking real."

"But it is," said Colette. "Say it, Marvin. Say it. This is real. I want to hear it."

Marvin felt the carpet beneath his fingers, the pain in his hip from slamming into the floor, the way his heart palpated thickly in his chest, and the sweat upon his brow. His nostrils were inundated with the sewage smell emanating from her. This had none of the hallmarks of a dream.

Maybe if I just do what she says, I can get out of this alive, he thought, then choked a laugh, *And then check myself in for a 72-hour hold.* His eyes traced her feet to her blazing eyes. He swallowed, reluctantly verbalizing what he wished to fight. "This is real."

Colette nodded. "Good boy."

Marvin sat up, cradling his face in his hands. *What the fuck is happening here*? The visitor blocking his exit stood like a commander, her stance at odds with her soaked sundress. Droplets of water fell from her body onto the carpet. At the sight, Marvin momentarily regained his nerve. "You're making a mess of my floor," he said, pointing.

"You made a mess of my life," retorted Colette.

Marvin shook his head. "I didn't do anything to you."

Colette's expression hardened, and she crept closer to Marvin on hands and knees. It took everything within Marvin not to creep backward, but to stand his ground. "You really think that?"

His jaw firm, Marvin nodded. He stared resentfully into Colette's eyes, and she met him with equal vitriol until her expression suddenly softened. She grinned.

"Fortunately, it doesn't matter much what you think. You have no power here." She stood, sashaying past him before settling herself into the armchair in the corner of his bedroom. Wet footprints followed her path, rekindling Marvin's anger.

"You're fucking up my house," he said.

Colette smiled all the more broadly. "It's the least of the pain and suffering you're about to experience, trust me."

"Then what do you want from me? As we've established, you're dead. You're done. Whatever you think I did to you, it's over."

"You see," said Colette, relaxing back into the chair, "I thought the same."

The squelchy sound of Colette's movements in the chair made Marvin squirm. He made to protest, but she continued.

"I thought I was done, too. Thought all my problems were unsolvable. Insurmountable. Thought I was worthless, couldn't make a difference, etcetera."

Marvin stood, his arms folded, taking in the sight of the bloody ghost in her flowery sundress curled into his chair. Hopefully, the smell wasn't permanent.

"I was wrong, though," said Colette. "Don't you have a blanket or something?"

Marvin frowned. "Can you get cold?"

"What a rude question. Hand me a blanket like a good boy."

Marvin threw up his hands in surrender. "Why not?" Maybe the sooner the spirit was sated, the sooner she would leave. He retrieved a scratchy, beige, sateen-bordered blanket from deep in his closet. He wasn't sure why he kept it anyway and reasoned he would be glad to toss it once Colette had finished with it. He threw it at her, keeping a good distance away.

"Ah-ah-ah," she said, tossing it back.

Marvin hesitated, then, with clenched teeth, obliged, draping the ugly blanket over the living corpse. He just wanted to go back to sleep, to get away from whatever this nightmare was.

"Thank you," said Colette, and Marvin stepped away. "I thought I was done for, too. And for a moment, I was. Before I departed for good, I learned of something of a business opportunity. I realized maybe I couldn't save myself—but then again, maybe my work had only begun."

"Your *work*," repeated Marvin.

"My work," she confirmed. "I've been given the chance to relieve a good deal of suffering in the world."

"What are you—"

"*Suffering*," Colette continued pointedly, "that you have inflicted upon others for way too long."

Marvin folded his arms. "I don't know what you're talking about."

"How about planning to sue my dad?"

He blanched momentarily. She had overheard his plans as he paced her apartment. "Fine, if you leave, I won't call your father."

Colette scoffed.

"I won't!" Marvin's eyes were wide with insistence, but he could only maintain it for so long before they narrowed once more. "Even though you left me a goddamn *mess* to deal with."

She snorted a laugh. "There it is."

"It's not free to clean up your remains," he pointed out.

Colette shook her head. "Maybe the money doesn't matter as much as being a decent person. Have you ever thought of that?"

"*Decent person.*" Marvin glowered. "Miss Finch, you signed a contract. You promised me, of your own free will, that you would,"—Marvin ticked his fingers, counting the points of the contract—"one, inhabit the apartment for 12 months and pay accordingly, and two, keep it in good condition. And three, if you failed to do so, you would pay for the damage." He scoffed, holding his arms out as though he had won. "What more do you want?"

Colette met Marvin's gaze. "If it were only about that, I wouldn't be here."

"You signed a contract," Marvin repeated matter-of-factly.

Colette stood, smacking the arms of the chair. "Fuck your contract and fuck *you*. It's not just about me."

Heat flushed through Marvin's body. He clenched and unclenched his fists before pointing to the door and shouting, "Get out!"

Colette struck like lightning, appeared before Marvin's face, her nose inches from his own. He jumped back, startled.

"Have you ever heard of karma, Marvin?" spat Colette, saliva landing upon Marvin's face. "You've always been free to choose your actions. But you've never had the freedom to choose the consequences, nor when they would come about."

He wiped the spittle away, then crossed his arms over his racing heart. "That's bullshit."

"Really."

"Yes."

"*Really.*"

Colette looked at Marvin with less anger now. Was she amused?

"Honestly, you being such an asshole only makes my job easier."

Marvin barked out a laugh which had a note of worry he would never admit to. "What job? What can you possibly do to me? You're *dead*."

"If I told you right now, this would become a lot less fun for me." Colette sighed, then walked around Marvin and back to her chair. Once she had tucked herself in—a sight which made Marvin involuntarily shudder—she crossed one putrid leg over the other and laid her hands upon her blanket-covered knee. "Money is not all that matters. I mean"—Colette gestured to the room—"what has it brought you? You, alone in this big house. No wife. No children.

Nothing. Not even a *dog*." She pursed her lips as though suppressing a smile.

With Colette out of his face, Marvin's bravado came more easily. "Are you here to argue philosophy, then? Is that what I'm in for? You'll bore me to death?"

"Oh, no. I don't believe you'll be bored." She giggled again, a sound Marvin decided he hated the most.

"What then? You're Marley's ghost with some kind of,"—he pointed to the black cuff around her ankle—"new-age chains." He raised his hands and wiggled his fingers in mockery of a spooky storyteller. "Three spirits will visit me tonight. Tomorrow I'll throw my money around because I've seen the error of my ways."

Marvin was about to add something about adding a replacement chair to the charge for the damage to her apartment when Colette actually threw back her head and laughed, a sound which made his bowels run cold. His vindictive thoughts were quelled by the sudden longing for her giggling.

"You think you're Ebenezer Scrooge here? You think you're just... what? Misunderstood? That I'll find something deep down inside that'll change you, then everything will be fine?"

What Marvin thought but wouldn't say was, *actually, yes*.

Colette's smile lost its mirth and took on malevolence. "I'm not convinced you've got anything good in you. You're a piece of shit. Full stop. Inside and out. I'm sure of it."

Ignoring her continued disrespect, Marvin argued, "If I'm no good, what's the point? What are you doing here?"

Colette drummed her fingers on the arm of the chair. "You're a mean one, Mr. Hoeff, but that isn't going to be the case anymore. Not if I have something to say about it."

She smiled again, her skin so pale that her lipstick looked more like blood than makeup. "And as you might have guessed, I do."

Colette sat in that chair, her eyes glued to Marvin's without wavering. A degree of panic set in his chest before it plummeted to his ass with fear. He could strong-arm an eskimo into buying an air conditioner, but he knew—as sure as he knew he would have to replace that chair tomorrow—that there was no getting around whatever Colette had in mind for him.

Even as he briefly considered making a run for the door, he recalled the swiftness with which Colette was able to move. The fact she was able to touch him.

Upon this reflection, Marvin's shoulders slumped. An old country song came to mind, something about how the only way through hell was, well, through. It seemed relevant advice at the moment.

He rubbed his face, then swallowed hard, acquiescing to whatever came next. "What now, then?"

Colette settled back, appearing pleased. "Finally. You've got it through your thick fucking head. You've got no power here."

"What are you going to do to me?"

The ghostly figure waved a hand casually, splashing a few drops of liquid upon the floor. "Oh, Marvin, don't look so scared. It's not that bad." She demurely covered the smile playing on her lips. "Well, not *really*."

Her smugness annoyed him deeply. Nonetheless, he shrugged. "Okay, then. Let's get this over with."

Colette clicked her tongue. "It's not like I need your permission."

"Of course not." He sighed.

Still, this implicit acceptance of his fate seemed to electrify Colette, who grinned as a child might before opening a long-awaited present. "That's what I was hoping for. Now settle in, Mr. Hoeff. It's going to be a wild ride."

Chapter Four

Marvin's world went dark. When it swam back into view, he sat in a chair behind a long, bare wooden desk. Before him was an open area, followed by dark oak paneling and a podium. On the wall behind the podium were tiny flags representing hundreds of countries. Marvin scanned the scene, which had all the appearances of a courtroom, including a robot which appeared to be functioning as a kind of bailiff off to one side.

Perplexed, Marvin turned to find Colette in the seat beside him.

"What—"

She raised a finger to her lips. "Shhh."

No longer dressed in the bloodied sundress, Colette wore a smart pantsuit, her hair pulled back in a tight bun. Her lips were as red as ever, but in a powerhouse attorney kind of way instead of Pennywise. Despite this refreshing change, Marvin frowned. He looked down to find that his outfit had changed from his pajamas to a dark blue suit. Marvin's eyes flashed with the implication.

"Did you *re-dress* me?" he hissed.

Before Colette could respond, the robot commanded in monotone, "All rise."

Marvin looked to Colette whose gesture implied he would be a moron not to do so. In his befuddlement with the situation, he found no reason not to comply. A man in black robes entered and took his place at the bench.

"Court is now in session." The judge pounded his gavel. "We're here today in the case of the people against Marvin Hoeff."

"Yes, your honor." The voice came from Marvin's right. He looked to see a blond woman he hadn't noticed before. "This is a bad one too."

"Hmm," said the judge noncommittally. He exuded boredom, and Marvin wasn't sure whether this was an advantage.

"You'll see all the evidence in front of you, your honor."

"Hmm. I see what you mean."

As these two had their discussion, Marvin had a realization. He looked at Colette. "Wait, are you my attorney?"

"Miss Finch, please maintain control of your client."

"I'm sorry, your honor," said Colette. She fixed Marvin with a look and put a finger to her lips before sliding a pen and notepad toward him. Marvin frowned. How could he expect Colette to be his attorney when she had such obvious derision for him? Instead of pursuing the point, he folded his arms and settled back into his chair to watch the proceedings.

The lawyer at the other desk continued speaking. "Your honor, I hate to say it, but I think we're wasting time here."

"We always are," the judge said with a chuckle.

"My client deserves a chance," said Colette.

"You have a conflict of interest," spat the other lawyer.

Hell yeah, *she does*, thought Marvin bitterly.

"What makes you think he'll change?" the other lawyer continued.

"Given the tools of the court, I know Mr. Hoeff can be persuaded. If you entrust him to my care, I can assure you, your honor, that he'll have the best chance to change."

Colette's apparent defense of Marvin befuddled him. What was she playing at?

The other lawyer scoffed, but Colette was undaunted. "That's the whole reason I'm here."

The judge sat behind his podium looking at something. Marvin figured they were some kind of legal documents until he made out the words on the cover: *USA Today Crosswords - Easy Fast and Fun Crossword Puzzles - Jumbo Issue.* His heart thudded in his chest.

"So, the classic PPF treatment?"

The what?

Colette scoffed. "Your honor, someone like Mr. Hoeff should go straight to the newly designed reformation chambers." Her lawyerly demeanor faltered for a moment when her lips pursed and a certain gleam of delight played in her eyes which unnerved Marvin. But the expression disappeared as quickly as it had appeared. "I believe that particular form of rehabilitation would give us—my client, that is—the best chance."

The judge looked at his crossword for another long moment before writing something down and looking at Colette over his glasses. "Well, if you're sure." He looked at the opposing counsel. "Do you have any objections?"

The opposing counsel shrugged. "I suppose it's mainly Miss Finch's time that will be wasted. I don't find these new methods persuasive, personally. I mean, the ankle monitor?" She pointed to the band around Colette's ankle, still visible around the leg of her pantsuit. "It doesn't have near the impact chains used to."

Marvin leaned back with slight satisfaction having assessed her ankle monitor correctly.

"Yeah, yeah. Your objection is noted. Not scary enough, mmh-mmm," said the judge with the air of one who had heard it all before. He turned his attention to Marvin and Colette once more. "Mr. Hoeff, please rise."

He obeyed, as did Colette beside him.

"Your lawyer recommends the reformation chambers. This is all voluntary, you understand, but the alternatives are less than ideal."

It's not real, he reminded himself. *None of this can be. This is all nonsense, some kind of fever dream. Even if it's a haunting.*

"What say you?" asked the judge.

"Sure," said Marvin. *Voluntary, my ass.*

"Bailiff, bring the defendant the first document." The judge replaced his glasses and returned to his crossword puzzle.

The robot bailiff wheeled itself before Marvin. A lengthy document printed from an opening in its belly and fell to the desk.

"Sign," said the robot.

"*Sign?*" Marvin balked as he took in the sheer volume of text on the document. What kinds of terms and conditions were hidden in there? He turned his attention to the judge. "I want to read it first."

"You will sign," the robot repeated.

The judge mumbled something without looking up from his puzzle and waved an indifferent hand in Marvin's direction. Marvin, beginning to sweat, tried to scan the document, but Colette nudged him before he could make out any words.

"You're really gonna want to sign this," she whispered.

"*What* am I signing?"

"Basically, you're agreeing to do the reformation chambers in order to save your soul, okay?"

He gawked at her, but she remained steady, one eyebrow raised in a challenge.

"You will sign," said the robot once more.

None of this is real, Marvin reminded himself. *It doesn't matter. Appease her and you'll be back home in your own bed before you know it. Add this to the pain and suffering you'll charge Mr. Finch for in the morning.*

"*O*-kay, as you wish," said Marvin, picking up a pen and signing on the line. "Whatever you say." Upon writing the last stroke, the robot snatched it. Another page printed from its belly, replacing the first sheet of paper.

"Sign the next."

"Now hold on just a minute," said Marvin. "How many more of these will there be? And what the hell, exactly, am I signing?"

"None of that language in my courtroom," replied the judge indifferently.

"Kangaroo fucking court," Marvin mumbled as he sat back against his chair and folded his arms. Even the robot looked aghast, though Marvin wasn't sure how.

Three sharp knocks of the gavel were audible. "Mr. Hoeff—" began the judge, but Colette cut in.

"Please excuse my client, your honor. This is an emotional time for him."

"I won't have this behavior in my court."

Colette gave Marvin a side-eyed threat. "He'll behave, your honor."

"He'd better," said the judge. "Or I'll hold you both in contempt."

"Yeah?" scoffed Marvin. "And what's that like?"

A chamber opened up behind the judge's chair with a blaze and a roar of fire. Even from 15 to 20 feet away, the heat warmed Marvin's face, making him wince away. He was forcibly reminded of the time he and a friend lit a bonfire using diesel fuel and burned their eyebrows clean off. They had been lucky to escape with no more serious injury. The door closed once more, and Marvin took a deep breath.

"What say you?" asked the judge.

Colette turned to Marvin, eyebrows raised. "You really don't want that, trust me. Get it together."

Even if he declined to accept the reality of this courtroom and the power it held, he had no desire to be exposed to the full effect of that heat. The diesel fire memory was unpleasant enough. Marvin sighed. "Yes, your honor." It took everything within him to keep his tone level.

With that, the documents kept printing from the belly of the robot bailiff until Marvin's wrist ached. He arched it, stretching it, and looked up with desperation for the papers to stop.

Another document printed and dropped upon the table, this one in font large enough to read. It was a checkbox-bulleted list.

"Select three," said the bailiff.

Marvin frowned. The list consisted of one-word nonsense, things like Squish, Feet, Reflex, Fur, Roast, Hang, Land, Bury, Purple, Red, Soft. He looked up past the bailiff to the judge. "That's it?" he asked.

"Unless you'd like more," the judge said with an eye roll.

Marvin nodded slowly. "So these are the reclamation chambers?"

"Reformation chambers," drawled the judge.

Marvin glanced at Colette. "What if I don't choose anything?"

The judge sighed. "Then Miss Finch has free rein to follow you the rest of your life."

"*What?*"

Colette giggled, then pressed her lips together. "It was in the paperwork," she whispered.

"Some attorney you are." Marvin glowered at Colette, then determined nothing could be worse than having Colette's spirit annoying him forever.

Nothing.

"Let's get this over with, then."

"You've made a wise choice, Mr. Hoeff," said the judge.

Marvin nodded dispassionately before consulting the list again, trying to choose the least offensive-sounding options. He found his hope of information and context dashed once more as he scanned the list of one-word descriptors.

Bug. Floss. Tissue. Baby. No categories. No explanations. The list wasn't even alphabetized.

What the hell did they mean? Marvin glanced up toward the judge, whose attention was back on the crossword puzzles. The robot was certain to provide no information. And he didn't exactly trust Colette.

Forget it, thought Marvin. The judge had instructed him to choose three. *At least three*, Marvin corrected. *As though anyone would ever choose more.*

Several options were immediately dismissed, such as Hang, Roast, and Bury. Squish didn't sound particularly enticing either, nor did Worm or Claw or Burn.

Marvin's gaze landed on Gold. He twiddled the pen between his fingers before shrugging and checking the box. It sounded at least preferable to Stake. One down, two more to go.

Prey? Nope.

Rope? Nada.

Grass? Maybe.

Haven. Now that sounded like a decent option, at least. Marvin checked that box too.

One more to choose, and the options seemed only bleaker.

Filth. Slob. Crush. Stomp. Skewer. Pike. One that simply said Papua New Guinea.

Jeez, they all sound pretty bad.

"Please choose quickly, Mr. Hoeff," said the judge. "This court has many cases to proceed with today."

Marvin glanced at the judge, then looked back at his sheet, trying to find anything that didn't sound awful. Roach? No. And not Mildew or Mold. What was the one that hadn't sounded terrible before? He scanned the list trying to jog his memory.

Then he saw Table and Home. Wanting to get it over with as quickly as possible, Marvin deliberated before choosing Home. It sounded rather benign compared to such delights as Rats and Roach.

"All right, I've made my choices. Gold, Haven, and Home." Marvin slid the paper to Colette. Colette looked them over for a moment before handing the paper to the robot bailiff.

"Thank you," she said.

The bailiff wheeled to the opposing counsel, holding the paper out for her to see. She nodded. The paper was then wheeled to the judge.

"I think you'll see all is in order," said Colette.

The judge glanced at the paper and handed it back. "Ahh, yup, that'll do it." He turned his gaze to Colette while handing the bailiff a small black box. As the bailiff wheeled itself to Colette and handed her what turned out to be a remote, the judge said, "Go ahead and take your client out of here. G'luck, Miss Finch."

Bang went the gavel, and Colette turned to Marvin with a grin that chilled him to the bone. "Well, let's get this reformation started, then."

The blood drained from Marvin's face. *Fuck*.

Chapter Five

Colette grinned, holding the remote up for Marvin to see. "Where to first?"

Marvin swallowed, collecting himself and hoping to appear unperturbed. "Dealer's choice, I guess." What did it matter so long as it was over quickly?

"*Goody!*" Colette embraced the remote in her hands. "Haven it is."

This exuberance and speed of her decision making startled Marvin.

"Wait—" he began, but it was too late. Colette had pressed one of the buttons.

The courtroom whooshed out of existence with a bluster of wind, and a new scene replaced it. Disoriented, Marvin fell, wincing in anticipation of his face hitting the desk before him. Instead, his hands and knees landed on hard ground.

Marvin opened his eyes, confused. The ground before him was made up of brown pebbles. He looked up to find he was beside a large tree. Several, actually. He narrowed his eyes. Were they trees? They were short, standing only a foot or two taller than he, and almost entirely smooth and featureless. Familiarity lingered at the edge of Marvin's mind, but he struggled to find context.

"What is this place?" asked Marvin. Before Colette answered, he let out a yelp of shock at the sight of his hands.

"What the *fuck*." Instead of the wrinkled, stout fingers Marvin was used to, his hands had elongated, pinkened, and the fingers now extended into sharp claws. His eyes followed his arm to wrists now covered in taupe fur. Instead of the suit he had worn in the courtroom, he was clothed only in that fur. His belly, while admittedly paunchy before, had become more so. His feet were elongated versions of his pink crypt-keeper hands.

He felt his face. Fur covered an elongated snout from which whiskers protruded, twitching at his touch. To confirm his suspicions, he reached down with a shaky hand and found a worm-like tail swishing side to side.

Marvin looked back and let out a squeak of horror. "Am I... a mouse?"

The missing context of his surroundings took shape all at once. Those bizarre smooth trees were blades of grass. The pebbles, pieces of dark soil. He looked behind himself to see a tall brick building. He also saw a dark brown mouse with beady, gleaming eyes. It was nibbling a nut. At Marvin's notice, the mouse took on something of a smile, with enough of the cunning he associated with Colette—and a hint of dimples marking the fur of its face.

"Is that . . . Are you a mouse too?"

"Can't let you have all the fun," said the Colette-mouse.

"But..." Marvin puzzled. "Why?"

With no particular urgency, the Colette-mouse gnawed the rest of the nut and gulped it down before answering.

"As your lawyer, I know a fair number of your dirty little secrets. All the things you've done wrong, from big to small, against the most powerful to the most innocent."

"The most innocent?" Marvin squeaked. "I'm not supposed to exterminate mice now? Come on," he said with a mousy chuckle. "I'm supposed to be the Dalai Lama now? I know I'm not the best guy, okay, but this seems a little far."

Colette tidied her whiskers with her paws. "Zeus," she said.

Marvin turned his ear to her, wondering if he'd heard correctly. "As in the lightning god?"

She shook her head. "As in the cat."

"What the fuck are you talking about?"

Colette studied her claws absently. "You must not have known his name."

Marvin threw up his paws. "Tell me all about it. I'm sure you will, anyway."

"Gladly." Colette sat upon the ground and looked at Marvin. "Zeus was the cat at Haven Hill apartments that liked to wander. The little tabby. Remember?"

He racked his brain. *Oh, Haven Hill. Haven.* That made sense now. But a cat? A tabby? Marvin thought for a moment, then squeaked a laugh of recognition. "Maybe," he admitted.

"Now you're getting it."

Marvin settled into his haunches and folded his little arms. "You're not supposed to have outdoor cats. Bad for the environment, or something, plus something might happen to them."

"Yes, and that's what you told the Harwood family, isn't it? *Something might happen to him.*"

Marvin tapped his temple angrily. "Does your special little recall ability happen to show you that damn cat pissing in all the flower beds? And using the sandbox at the playground as its own personal litter box? It was a menace."

Marvin paused as the ground beneath him rumbled, then stopped.

Rumbled, then stopped.

He dug his claws into the earth in panic as the intermittent rumbles continued. "What is that?"

Instead of answering the question, Colette continued, "*Something might happen to him*, you said." Her eyes darkened. "And then you *made* something happen to him, didn't you?"

With his eyes fixed on Colette, Marvin didn't see the blow coming. A harsh thump to the left side of his ribs knocked him to the ground. He looked up and met a pair of electric green eyes, their pupils enlarged with violent playfulness.

Zeus. Oh no.

"*Prrb?*" purred Zeus.

Colette sat where she was, unperturbed as she watched Marvin set himself upright.

Shit, thought Marvin.

"Well, you solved that problem," said Colette. "You made sure he wouldn't piss anywhere near you anymore."

Marvin shook as he looked into the cat's eyes. The cat was still, except for its swishing tail.

Colette continued, "You made *sure* of that by taking him on a little road trip an hour away and leaving him there."

Zeus drew closer to Marvin, looming over him like the unyielding god for whom he was named. Marvin remained frozen aside from the uncontrollable shaking in his limbs. His heart pounded. He didn't know if mice could sweat, but was pretty sure he was sweating, nonetheless.

Unable to move, Marvin pled his case. "I dropped him in a neighborhood, okay? It's not like I ran him over with my car."

"No, you didn't. But little Zeus was so scared, so desperate to get to the little boy he belonged to that he *did* get hit by a car."

Marvin risked a look at Colette—a bad move, as it turned out, for this time, Zeus battered his right side, knocking him off his feet once more.

"You killed him, Marvin, as certainly as if you had driven the car yourself."

Marvin looked wildly around as he tried to stand up. The cat pounced, crushing Marvin beneath his paws. His breath left him in a *whoosh*. Meanwhile, the cat did that little playful *prrbt* sound again, something which Marvin was sure would echo in his nightmares for the rest of his life.

If, indeed, he got out of this situation alive—which was far from a foregone conclusion. Marvin had been reduced to a plaything in Zeus's paws, of no more significance than a catnip toy. His face pressed against the soil as the cat pinned him in place.

While Marvin fought for his life, Colette continued her lecture, "His owner cried and cried. He made missing posters and prayed every night for his best friend to come home. When his mom sat him down to explain he never would, he was heartbroken."

Marvin dug his paws into the dirt and attempted to pull. To his surprise, a break in the cat's grip allowed him to wriggle free and make a run for it.

Colette called after him, running to keep up. "He was only eight years old, and you took his best friend away. You broke his heart, Marvin."

Marvin hauled ass to a nearby drainpipe and slid beneath as if for home base. "Okay, okay," he panted. "I get it. Can we go now?"

"No, we can't."

A dark paw came swiping beneath the drainpipe, its claws extending like talons. One nearly caught Marvin's foot. He leaped back, pressing himself against a brick. "Please, why?"

"Because Zeus may be the god of thunder, but I am God of this world." She spoke in all earnestness but broke into giggles at the end of her sentence.

Another swipe of the paw, this time with claws extended, connected with Marvin's thigh. He gasped as pain surged. Blood gushed from the wound on his furry flank.

"Please, Colette?"

She didn't answer. Marvin whimpered, then started to weep, terrified. He found himself shaking, sitting in a pool of his own urine. The cat *prrped* another meow of excitement.

"Oh my God," Marvin moaned.

"I am the landlord now, Marvin, and you get to play by my rules," Colette laughed.

Marvin pressed himself as far back under the drainpipe as possible. Still, he had to leap over one of the paws that came swishing through. Colette was going to kill him. She was going to murder him with this furry creature.

If he survived this, Marvin swore he'd drop a lot more cats on opposite sides of town. Filthy, nasty—

Marvin screamed as another claw pinned his tail into place.

"The thing is, you've gotten used to being in charge. You think you're so important. Nothing else matters. Cats. Little boys. Other people, their needs and feelings. You're so out of touch that you think these things are beneath you, expendable. They're not. They matter. And the whole point of this is for you to learn that."

"Okay, okay, I've learned it. Can we go now?" yelled Marvin as he turned to the wall of the building and began trying to scramble up, but his claws found no purchase.

Colette, unmoved, continued, "Zeus's owner wasn't stupid. When the pound explained they had found a dead cat with a microchip belonging to them, he knew Zeus would never have gone that far. He knew someone had to bring him there."

The claw pinning his tail dragged him steadily out from beneath the drainpipe.

"You destroyed him, Marvin. You ruined his innocence, his belief that the world was good and people were kind."

Two paws came swishing beneath the drainpipe and hooked themselves painfully into his already wounded leg. Marvin screamed his pain and terror.

"And you won't be done here until I say you're done."

A sob escaped Marvin as he was dragged backward from his hiding place. "Colette, please, *please* stop this."

Pulled out from beneath the drainpipe, Marvin saw Colette. She sat atop the curved metal with placid interest as sharp teeth sank into his side.

"You can't treat people like garbage and get away with it forever, Marvin."

Marvin screamed as the teeth chomped down again and again. "*Please*!"

His bones were snapping, crunching sickeningly between Zeus's sharp teeth.

His legs.

His ribs.

His breath was knocked out of him, then failed to return. Did Zeus puncture his lung?

Another pain. Maybe his kidneys? His liver? It hardly mattered. Everything hurt.

Then Zeus enclosed his back between his teeth. With another crunching sound, Marvin felt a trickling liquid from his spine to his crumpled legs. The pain within came to an abrupt halt.

Marvin was paralyzed, literally this time. He could only look on as those bright green eyes looked at him with ravenous intensity. The eyes of Zeus were nearly entirely black, the pupil was so wide.

"*Please*," begged Marvin.

The intervening moments were like an eternity, waiting, wondering what Zeus would do. What Colette would allow. Surely she couldn't actually kill him, right? He still had two more of those reclamation things to go.

This couldn't be how he died.

Marvin caught sight of Colette. She sat twirling one of her whiskers, then heaved a sigh and crossed her furry legs.

"Oh, *fine*," she relented with the roll of her eyes. "Don't play with your food, Zeus."

Marvin let out a sigh of relief until he heard:

"Finish him."

His world went dark and a scorching pain encircled his throat as he screamed.

Oh, God, I'm being decapitated.

The pain was ferocious, and the terror reached a fever pitch as his scream was forcibly cut away.

Everything went black.

Chapter Six

Marvin came to slowly, then all at once, his hands grasping his throat to check whether it was in one piece or not. He looked down to see he was in normal clothing, even shoes. His hands were no longer those of a mouse.

He was still alive. His head was still attached. He wasn't bleeding, broken, bruised, or paralyzed. "It was just a dream. Just a dream," he said to himself.

"Not really," answered Colette.

Marvin turned to the source of the voice, rage boiling. She was no longer a mouse and now stood upon a balcony above his head. She leaned nonchalantly against the railing, still wearing that same stained sundress as before. "What the hell was that?"

"Congratulations, Marvin! You finished the first of your three reformation chambers."

Marvin stared. "Y-you're *psychotic*. You're insane. What the *hell* is happening here?"

"A hell of your own creation," Colette said with that same Cheshire-cat smile. "In the meantime, why don't you look around?"

Marvin glowered. "No thanks."

Colette shrugged. "It makes no difference to me. Take your time."

Marvin narrowed his eyes. "You killed me."

"You look well and alive to me."

"You know what I mean."

Colette laughed. "We can discuss this all day, if you want. It literally makes no difference to me."

Marvin turned away, chagrined, then caught sight of the surrounding room. He stood at the very center of what resembled the ballroom of some kind of Victorian mansion. The walls, the ceiling, and even the floors were gilded. Piled in the far end of the room was currency of all kinds: stacked bills still in wrappers from the bank and gold coins piled like fall leaves.

His breath caught at the sight. Could he... *swim* in them? Like Scrooge McDuck? He wanted to. It would be like living his ultimate childhood dream.

He felt Colette studying him, and so cleared his throat, arranging his expression into one of indifference. "I suppose this is Gold, then?"

"Beautiful, isn't it?" said Colette.

Marvin eyed her carefully before responding, "Well, *yes*. Better than the other place so far."

Colette smiled innocently. "No Zeus here, Marvin. You're right."

He rolled his eyes. "Yeah, yeah. What's the catch?"

"No catch, Marv. You're just in a room full of riches." The last word caught on a poorly disguised giggle. "What could happen?"

"Of course." Marvin huffed, rolling his eyes. "Why make it easy?"

"That would be boring," Colette annoyingly agreed.

Marvin decided to stop talking and ignore her for now. Whatever would happen was going to happen. He needn't let her enjoy the process too much.

He gazed around the room. "So whose money is this?"

"It's yours."

"What do you mean?"

"I mean, all that money you usually see in the form of digits in your bank account is here. Look at it all. Look what you've *earned*."

Her undisguised venom rankled Marvin. "I *have* earned it. I worked hard for all that."

Colette nodded with mock awe. "Wow."

"There's nothing wrong with having money," Marvin snapped.

Colette sighed. "No, not inherently. But maybe there's something wrong with earning it selfishly, then squirrelling it away, never helping anyone besides yourself."

"It's mine. I don't have to share it."

"But maybe you should."

Marvin scoffed. "So is that it? Gold is just you lecturing me on the philosophy of money in a room full of it? This is pathetic."

Colette flushed, then recovered. "If you're so impatient, why don't you poke around a bit? Do what your heart tells you, darling."

"My heart tells me to tell you to suck a fuck."

"Oh, Marv. Cool it with the sweet talk."

Marvin glowered as he stared at Colette's sparkling expression. "Fine. Okay. I'm doing what my heart tells me."

What his heart told him, his first instinct, was to collect as much of the stuff as he could before he was cast out. Maybe he could bring it with him and somehow double-dip his own cash supply. With a shrug, he reached out for the nearest bundle of fifties. Just as his fingers wrapped around it and he was reaching for the next, he screamed.

It squirmed. What dropped out of Marvin's hand was not the cash he had picked up, but a large green and white spider. Horrified, Marvin looked at the rest of the money around him. It looked like the gold coin swim was out of the question.

"Look at what you've earned!" Colette called out. "Bug money."

Marvin glared up at her. Colette responded with an eerie smile. Marvin was determined to hold his ground. She and the judge might be able to force him into this room with magical bug money, but they couldn't push him around any more than that. He didn't have to take this.

"I'm not touching any more of it," he said.

"That's fine," said Colette, gesturing behind him. "You can just wait for it."

Marvin turned around and was horrified to see the coins he had imagined swimming in had sprouted eight legs. A thousand golden spiders swarmed in his direction. They would be beautiful if not so very, well, spidery.

"*Shit*," he yelled, running for the far wall.

A door. Marvin needed to find a door. There had to be one, didn't there? Though a little voice told him to get it over with, hadn't he almost escaped Zeus under the drainpipe? It couldn't hurt to try. He scanned the wall, but found himself sinking. He looked back toward Colette, who had now risen higher above him.

How?

He looked down and realized the floor was not only lowering, but becoming slanted—like a funnel, not an elevator. He tried to keep his footing against the angle of the floor and the rising tide of spiders around him. "Colette, please."

"Money is a terrible master but an excellent servant. It's become your master. It's everything to you, but in the end, it means nothing."

"That's bullshit."

"It doesn't mean anything if you don't do anything with it. You look at the dollar amount in your bank as the end goal, the way in which you can tell everyone how much better you are. How much more hard-working. More loving. More worthy. More valuable."

Marvin was at a loss, because he did feel that way. Was he not more valuable? He could literally point to the value that proved it. He kicked more spiders off himself, though it seemed a fool's errand at this point. He just wished the spiders would go away. In the meantime, there was no point allowing Colette to see him falter. "What's wrong with making money? At least I'm making an honest living."

Colette let out a barky laugh. "*An honest living?*"

"I'm not begging," said Marvin as he waved his hands wildly trying to find something, anything to resist falling into the mass of spiders. He found only more spiders. What would happen when he fell? He swallowed hard. "I'm not stealing. Should I make less just so people don't feel bad about it?"

"You're just a businessman, providing people with the things they need. Taking care of them. Giving them a place to live. You're practically Mother Theresa." Colette rolled her eyes.

"If I didn't someone else would. Why shouldn't I?"

"Okay, but how you're living, is it the same as someone who spent what they needed, then used the rest to help others? Or—Christ," she slammed her hands upon the banister. "To take a woman out on a date once in a while? Maybe pay for a wedding and a couple of kids? Even a *dog* would be preferable, Marvin, but you have no one. You have only . . . those guys." She gestured to the golden spiders rising upon him like the water of the Titanic.

"I don't want any of that," said Marvin as staunchly as he could under the circumstances.

"Then your money in the real world is as meaningless as it is here. You need to learn. You need to change. You can't be a selfish bastard anymore. Too much is at stake."

"Like what?" Marvin was really sliding now.

"Have you ever heard of the butterfly effect?"

"Butterfly flaps its wings, tornado happens across the world. Sure."

"You're the butterfly."

"This is bullshit," Marvin said, swatting away more pursuing spiders. "Can we just finish this up? Let's finish my punishment and go home."

"As you wish," said Colette. She looked somewhere behind herself. "He's all yours."

Marvin gasped in shock as the floor gave way beneath his feet and he fell, thumping into a pile of wriggling golden spiders. "You crazy *bitch*!" he yelled.

"I hope you're taking this seriously, Marvin, because if you don't do this correctly, you're stuck with me."

Before he could think much on this statement, Marvin was pulled beneath the fathoms of spiders. He sucked for breath and received no air for his trouble, only a scratchy feeling like a tiny tumbleweed. Turning his head away in disgust, he found no comfort, only more spiders. He had no air left in his lungs. The spiders crawled down his throat and into his airway.

His final thought was a vow to squish every single spider he came across from that point forward.

Chapter Seven

Marvin groaned and rolled over, coming to consciousness slowly. He put his hands under his pillow.

His *pillow*.

His eyes opened, and he looked around himself. Relief flooded his aching spirit as he took in the sight of his own sheets, his pillow, his nightstand, his bedside. He was in his room. Light filtered around the edge of his curtains to signal the start of a new day.

Court, the cat, his decapitation, his drowning in a sea of spiders, it had all been a nightmare.

Marvin snorted a laugh. *What a night.* The birds twittered outside as he rubbed his eyes. It was just another day. Just another very normal, not cursed day, and Marvin's indigestion-fueled nightmare was blessedly over.

But when he rolled over, there laid Colette. "Good morning, darling."

Marvin groaned and turned back over. "Haven't I been through enough?"

"What? You're home."

He barked a laugh. "But there's a catch, right? Like the bed's going to grow teeth and eat me, or the shower is going to trap me and, I don't know, scald my skin off or something."

Colette shrugged. "Solid ideas, but no, none of those."

Marvin sighed, then sat up. "All right. Whatever. Let's get this over with."

"Oh now, that's not a good attitude to have."

Marvin drummed his fingers.

Colette smiled. "I can do this all night, you know. Time doesn't matter much to me anymore."

"Fine. So it's time to get ready for work, then?"

"Yes, Marvin, just a nice, normal morning. So why don't you go ahead and get yourself dressed and ready for your day?"

Marvin rolled his eyes. "Well sure, Colette, I would love to."

As he might on any other morning, a morning on which he was alone, not joined by a spectral pest, Marvin rolled out of his bed and stood. He jostled his weight between his feet, testing the floor. It didn't collapse under his weight. It seemed a good start.

Still when he stepped forward, he did so tentatively, his eyes narrowed at Colette, but her expression gave nothing away.

He opened the door of the closet with trepidation for potential danger, forcefully reminded of the old trick can full of snakes, but none seemed evident.

Marvin looked over his clothing options. What does one wear for a voyage through purgatory?

"What should I wear?" asked Marvin.

"Maybe that nice teal shirt. Or green. Seems, I don't know, plucky."

"Thanks." He started to grab for the teal shirt, then glared at Colette before choosing the orange sweater next to it. He then grabbed the first pair of pants he came across, some black slacks.

He turned to dress, then paused. "Mind turning around or something?"

Colette covered her eyes with her hand, giggling, and Marvin rolled his eyes. *It doesn't matter, anyway. Who gives a shit if she sees your skivvies? She's dead.*

Dressed in this unintentionally Halloween-y ensemble, Marvin turned around and held his hands out. "Good enough?"

"Socks?"

Marvin harrumphed. He retrieved some from his drawer, balancing on one foot at a time to put them on. "My shoes are downstairs, though."

"Then be my guest," said Colette, extending one pale arm as if in invitation to the rest of the house.

"It's *my* house," snapped Marvin.

"I'm in charge here, remember?"

"Yeah, yeah." Marvin mimed tipping his hat to her with a cold expression on his face. *Whatever gets this over with.* "What now, then, Your Highness?"

"That's more like it. Okay, Marv. It's your day off. It's time to relax, to enjoy yourself. What are you going to do first?"

He shrugged. "I guess I'll eat breakfast."

"Delightful. Did you know you can have whatever you like?"

Marvin was about to protest again, then gritted his teeth. "Why thank you."

"My pleasure."

Marvin headed out the door and down the stairs to his kitchen. He had a few breakfast sandwiches in the freezer that sounded good. His stomach rumbled. In fact, they sounded great.

"As I was saying, you can have whatever you like this morning." Colette bounded before him gleefully. "I think you'll like what we have to offer."

"We?"

The question was soon answered. Marvin entered the kitchen to find a woman standing before a hot stove. The smell of country-style gravy met his senses. Despite his justifiable suspicion of Colette's motives, he salivated. Biscuits and gravy sounded far better than a freezer sandwich.

The chef turned with a smile. She was middle-aged and portly with red hair pulled back into a bun. "What can I get you to drink?" Her speech was thick with what Marvin believed to be a French accent.

Marvin glanced at Colette before answering, "Orange juice."

An elbow met Marvin's ribs.

"What's the magic word?" whispered Colette.

He glared at Colette like a sullen child. "Orange juice, *please*."

"Yes, sir, coming right up," promised the chef. "Anything for you, *ma cherie*?"

Colette giggled. "A mimosa, please."

The chef nodded. "Of course, of course." She turned away.

Colette touched Marvin's arm, a gesture from which he recoiled. She appeared not to notice. "Isn't this nice?"

"Sure," said Marvin, settling himself a bit further away from her.

"No, but really. You've got a lovely home. And a personal chef! Lovely. Lovely, lovely, lovely."

Every passing moment left Marvin more uncertain, unsure what Colette was playing at. It was hard not to immerse himself in the comforts of home, with the smell of homemade breakfast wafting before him. Was it laced with something? He hardly had time to venture down this line of thinking before a plate of biscuits smothered with rich gravy was placed before him. Scrambled eggs and perfectly bite-sized pieces of cantaloupe soon joined on another plate.

"And your *jus d'orange*," said the chef.

"Thank you," he said, glancing pointedly at Colette.

"You're very welcome. *Bon appétit!*" She set a large glass with a spiralized orange peel on its rim before Colette. "And for you, *mademoiselle*."

"*Merci*," said Colette with a demure tip of her head. She turned to Marvin. "Oh, she's very good, isn't she?"

"She is," said Marvin. He dug into his food with abandon. After the adventure of the evening, he could eat this helping and more. He deserved it. He snarfed down several bites of food before raising the orange juice to his lips and washing it all down.

Heavenly. The best meal he had ever had, in fact. If this was his punishment, he would happily stay here for the rest of time.

He had all but lost himself in the enjoyment, placing another fork full of the stuff into his mouth, when Colette spoke again.

"Yes, home is very important. It's very important to feel safe and comfortable and cared for in your own home," she said. "Everyone deserves that."

Marvin frowned, watching her as he chewed and swallowed the bite in his mouth. "Yes, that's true."

Colette took another sip of her mimosa.

"Could I bring you any more, sir?" asked the chef.

Marvin met her gaze. It was full of sincerity, making him slowly bob his head. "Yes, please."

He turned back to Colette, curious. The chef spoke. "Here you are, sir."

When Marvin turned to face the chef again, he nearly fell off his stool. "What the *fuck*?"

"What is it, dear?" asked Colette.

Marvin gagged on the bit of food left in his mouth. The food on the plate in front of him was far different from what he had been eating before. Rather than the creamy white gravy with dark flecks of deliciously moist, seasoned pork sausage, a greenish black-flecked slime covered the plate.

Mold. It was moldy.

"Is there something wrong?" asked the chef. Marvin turned his horrified gaze to her but found no helping hand. Instead, the chef's face had similarly rotted, like a very old corpse during the height of summer. He inhaled a high-pitched scream which was barely audible but unable to be contained.

He threw down his fork and turned to Colette. "I knew it. I fucking *knew* it."

"It is not good?" the chef asked.

Without responding, Marvin stalked from the kitchen with its rotten food and decomposing chef into the living room. He couldn't take much more from Colette and the judge and the whole tour-de-freak he was on this evening.

On his way to the living room, however, a line of cockroaches barreled past him. Not the big nasty kind, which would be bad enough, but the insidious little German ones.

He leaped over them in an awkward kind of grand jete and landed on the carpet of the living room. He immediately wished he hadn't, for grouped there was a nest of mice he'd rudely interrupted with his entrance.

"It's awful when a place where you should feel safe turns on you," Colette said from somewhere behind him.

Marvin turned on his heel. "I've never poisoned anyone. I've never put roaches in their house. This isn't relevant to me."

"You think so?"

"I *know* so," he argued.

"What about that tenant that complained about roaches, and you told them they were dirty and had to deal with the problem themselves?"

"I gave them a roach motel."

"Yeah, *one*. One measly trap. As they say, if you see one, think thousands."

"It says in the lease they signed it's not my problem."

"But Marvin, it was."

"You don't know anything." Marvin, not wanting to back down even though he wasn't sure of what her plans were, made his way to the stairs. He scaled them as usual, but something was different. When his head slammed into the ceiling after the fifth step, he realized it had been an illusion. "The fuck?"

He frowned at this development, looking back toward the living room where more rats and roaches than before gathered. Colette, much to his chagrin, stood at the bottom of the steps with one of the rats sitting in her hand. She stroked its head with grotesque tenderness.

"People should feel safe at home," said Colette. "They shouldn't be given shoddy repairs and extorted for increasingly expensive rent."

"I keep all my units up to standard," said Marvin.

Colette raised the hand in which the rat was sitting. "Rats."

Marvin huffed. "None of my units have a rat problem."

"Not what I'm talking about. It's what you call your tenants when you think no one's listening." She cuddled the rat like a baby and used one hand to cover its ears. "You'd call them dirty, stinking, good-for-nothing, filthy, disease-spreading, sub-human rats." She uncovered the rat's ears. "Not that I think that about them. But that's what you've said."

"How would you know that?" Marvin asked.

"What an awful thing to say about people," Colette said, not bothering to respond to the question. "If you really feel that way, then do you keep your units up to people standard or rat standard?"

"*Jesus.* You don't know anything about my line of work."

"Those *rats* are paying for your investments, Marvin. For your mortgage. For all the stupid shit you ever bought. It came from your tenants working their asses off at jobs that don't pay enough. Meanwhile, you'd sit on your ass and do nothing. Care for nobody. Be nobody. Yes, of course, Marvin, *they're* the rats. *They're* the worthless pieces of shit, not you."

Marvin stomped back down the stairs, ready to blow a gasket when his foot went through the floor. "You don't know what it's like! Every moment, there's someone who wants to take advantage of me, of my money, of my units. I have to be ready for all kinds of bullshit people pull. Do you have any idea what that's like?"

"Maybe not," said Colette, "but I know that people matter. It matters that people have a home, somewhere they feel safe, not a place they feel can be pulled away at any moment, that can become unsafe, unlivable. They should have a home where the floors and walls and ceilings are taken care of properly, where they feel safe to come home, where they don't dread being because it feels like a *prison* but one they have to *pay for*."

The venom in her voice took Marvin by surprise, throwing him momentarily. She took advantage of his silence to continue.

"You selfish *monster*. And then you turn around and come after my dad. What a monstrous, selfish thing to do. Like really? His daughter just died," she spat.

Marvin was unmoved. Instead, his eyes flashed. "Well, gee, I wonder who killed her."

Colette balked. Sensing weakness, Marvin locked in. "You talk a good game about how selfish I am, but what about you? If you're so worried about your father, why would you take his daughter away? Who's really the monster here?"

Colette's expression darkened. "I'd watch what you say."

"No, why should I?" laughed Marvin. "What are you going to do to me? Feed me to an alligator? Send me back to the ice age to freeze to death? None of it's real, Colette. None of it." He folded his arms in triumph, smiling for the first time. "And to my recollection, I'm done here. I've finished my punishment."

Colette stilled. "And that's it." She paused, meeting his gaze. "You've learned nothing."

"I guess not."

She glared at him for a long moment. Her expression softened a bit, but with something more like despair than relief. "I'm your lawyer, Marvin. Remember? I didn't think you'd change, but that doesn't mean the fun has to stop."

Marvin's home, Halloween outfit, nice sheets, bedroom, and everything else disintegrated once more in favor of another, surely less enjoyable place.

As the darkness came once more, Marvin heard Colette spit one more, "Asshole."

The long wooden desk, the oak paneling, the podium, the tiny flags, the robot bailiff, they were all back. Marvin's outfit was no longer the orange and black getup, but the suit as before.

He sighed. "Oh, Colette, I know this is a kangaroo court to the highest degree, but I've done my whole punishment, haven't I?"

Colette shook her head and put a finger to her lips, then pointed to the judge, who rolled his eyes and pounded his gavel.

"Order, order." He leaned upon the podium. "I thought we were finished, Miss Finch?"

"If I may, Your Honor," said Colette. She cleared her throat. "Even though my client has completed his prescribed course through the reformation chambers, I don't believe it's been effective."

The judge raised an eyebrow. "No?"

Colette shook her head, her hands crossed before her. "No, Your Honor. You mentioned the PPF treatment before. At the time, I worried such a thing was too . . . soft, I suppose, for my client. But I wish to ask, is that option still on the table?"

Marvin looked worriedly at Colette. If the three previous torments were unpleasant, he wasn't sure what to expect from the PPF treatment. Maybe it wouldn't be so bad though, if she thought it was soft. *She's just pissed off. This is a Hail Mary. It'll be over soon.*

The judge peered over his glasses down at Colette, studying her for a moment before settling back into his chair. "Bailiff, will you please make a note of Miss Finch's report that the reformation chambers seem ineffective? That's valuable feedback."

An electronic melody followed, to which the judge responded, "Thank you." He closed his crossword puzzle and leaned forward on it, looking at Marvin. "Mr. Hoeff, thank you for participating in our experimental program. With the influx of new cases, we're trying some new techniques. . . but maybe the old timers had their reasons."

Marvin frowned, wondering how often this sort of thing happened.

The judge sighed, leaning back against his chair and speaking to no one in particular. "Change can't be forced, unfortunately. All we can do is our best." He looked to Colette once more. "Now, Miss Finch, this is your last chance."

She nodded.

"But if you think it would help, I'll oblige." He sighed. "PPF treatment, so ordered." The gavel pounded once more, and, once more, Marvin was whisked away for whatever gentler treatment this so-called PPF treatment called for.

Chapter Eight

THE COURTROOM WINKED OUT of existence. Marvin stared at its replacement: the wood-paneled wall, the mustard yellow flower-patterned drapes which clashed harshly with the green and orange patterned wallpaper surrounding it, and the orange shag carpet which was long enough to need mowing.

It was a place Marvin knew well: his childhood bedroom.

He had been transported back to the seventies, back before cell phones or the Internet, to the room where he had read comics and dreamed about girls.

Nodding as he added it all up, he said, "The old timers. The past. PPF. Past, present, future."

Colette nodded. "A classic."

Marvin raised an eyebrow at the way she sounded less cocky than before, but had little time to contemplate, before a piercing screech reached his ears. Alarmed, he turned to Colette, but she wasn't meeting his gaze—only glaring at the door with her arms folded.

The screeching continued alongside a rhythmic thumping—stomping footsteps, he soon discovered—followed shortly by an exasperated female voice.

"Just because you *want it* doesn't mean you can *have it*."

"Mother." Marvin spoke the word with longing, his eyes widened as he looked about.

He was momentarily distracted by the smaller version of himself running toward him. Marvin had no time to leap out of the way and prepared to have the wind knocked from him like Zeus had done before, but it never came. His young counterpart ran right through him before throwing his tiny body onto his bed, fists balled, beating on the pillow.

Marvin touched his abdomen where his younger self had passed through. *Bizarre.* It was so bizarre, in fact, it temporarily distracted him from the dread of what was to come, a memory which caused Marvin to long for the delights of Haven once more.

He shook his head. "I don't want to watch this."

Colette looked at him, eyebrow raised. Arrogance crept back into her expression. "Well, we're not leaving."

The scene before them unfolded with persistence.

"Marvin, that's enough."

The woman whisked past the ghostly pair to her son's bedside. Present-Day Marvin's hand settled over his heart as he watched her longingly. She pushed her hair, lighter blond than he remembered, back over her shoulder and crossed her arms. The child beside her gnashed his teeth in rage.

She sighed heavily, then reached out a hand. "Give it to me."

Young Marvin looked up from his bed with a set jaw and hard eyes. "No."

"Marvin, I said *give it to me.*"

"*No.*"

The mother seethed. As she glared into her son's blazing eyes, the wheels in her mind seemed to turn, trying to find some kind of purchase in the argument.

She sucked her teeth. "Marvin, I swear, if you don't give me that game right now . . ." Her lips remained parted, but no threat crossed them.

Even though Present-Day Marvin was a grown man in some kind of forced hallucination, he looked far more uncomfortable than his contemporary self.

"Please, I don't want to watch this," said Present-Day Marvin.

"Even more reason to stay," said Colette, her eyes remaining fixed on the scene before her. Her expression told Marvin it was beyond fighting. He ran his fingers through his hair and crossed his arms.

Young Marvin turned to glare at his mother. "Fine. It's just a stupid game, anyway." The boy withdrew a bright pink box from beneath his pillow and threw it near his mother's feet. It lay face-up and Marvin was able to read the title: *Circus Atari*.

The woman followed its arc through the air with pursed lips until it hit the floor near her feet. "I'm going to choose to ignore for a moment the fact that you threw that at me. I'm not raising a thief, young man. When are you going to learn that it's *not all about you?*"

The boy winced as if slapped. "All about me?" he asked. "Really?"

"Really. Stealing is so wrong. It's such a selfish thing."

His mouth fell open in outrage, but he closed it again and looked away from his mother, glaring at an indistinct spot on the wall.

The woman kneeled to pick up the game, shaking her head, then stood up, waving the game at the boy. "I don't get it. I just don't get it. You don't even *have* an Atari, Marvin. Why would you do this?"

"You don't get it," Young Marvin mumbled.

His mother turned her ear toward him with an eyebrow raised. "What was that?"

Young Marvin looked at her steadily and spoke as though explaining something to a small child. "I said, *you don't get it.*"

The mother pressed her lips together, both eyebrows now in danger of disappearing into her hairline. "Young man—"

"Just leave me alone!" roared Young Marvin, his hands balled into fists.

The mother slammed her hand against the door frame. "Marvin, I don't know what to do with you anymore. I don't know why you're so angry."

Young Marvin threw himself onto his bed again and rolled toward the wall. "Just leave me alone. You have the game. Just—just go."

"Marv—"

"*Go away!*"

The woman massaged her temples and took a long breath before letting it out shakily. "I don't know what to do with you anymore. I really don't."

She looked at her son for one last long moment, then turned and exited, shutting the door behind her. The boy within broke down into sobs.

On the sidelines of the scene, Present Day Marvin stood with his arms folded and jaw set as he stared at the floor. From the corner of his eye, he saw Colette look his direction.

"So, I'm wondering . . . Why *would* you steal a game you couldn't play?" she asked.

Present-Day Marvin rubbed his face in much the same way his mother had.

Colette continued looking at him. "You know I won't leave you alone. I won't go away. You can't make me, so you might as well tell me."

Marvin looked at her for a long moment. "I treated her terribly. I was such a little shit."

"You still are," said Colette.

"Just stop," Marvin snapped. "Do you really want to know? *Really?* Because I think I'd rather spend a few more rounds with Zeus than do this."

"When you put it that way, yes, I really want to know."

Marvin glared at her, then took a deep breath and let it out before speaking. "My friend knew a kid who knew my stepbrother. He told me that my dad gave him an Atari for his birthday."

Colette frowned. "So?"

"He got an Atari for his birthday from *my* dad. Not his dad. *Mine.*" Marvin laughed without humor. "Know what he gave me?"

"What?"

Marvin looked directly at Colette and touched the tips of his thumb and forefinger together in an O-shape. "Nothing."

Colette frowned. "Oh."

"It was *always* like that. My father hardly recognized my existence. Stealing the game . . . I don't know." Marvin trailed off, watching his younger self sniffle into his pillow. "I can't explain it. I got so goddamned mad." He sighed. "I guess I wanted to feel important. *For once.*"

Colette studied him for a long while.

Long enough that Marvin was compelled to ask, "What?"

She shook her head. "That's a pretty shitty thing for him to do," she said.

"I didn't know how to tell my mom that's why I did it. It sounded stupid."

"Do you want to know what she did after this?" asked Colette.

Not really, thought Marvin, and yet part of him wondered.

Before he could answer, Colette led the way out of the bedroom to leave the young Marvin to his own devices. Marvin followed, morbid curiosity overriding self-preservation.

They followed the sound of sobbing into a violently yellow and orange kitchen. Marvin's mother sat at the round dark wood dining table with her head in her hands. Tears spilled down her face.

Marvin reached out to touch her back, to comfort her. When his hand passed through, his own eyes glistened. "My dad wasn't around to get mad at. It was just my mom. So she got everything he should have gotten." Marvin chuckled a bit, then sniffled. "Her reward for raising me on her own, I guess."

Colette looked on wordlessly, studying the scene.

Marvin closed his eyes. "I wish I could take it back. I wish I'd known how little time I'd have with her. I never . . . I never apologized for what an ass I was."

Sobbing subsided to sniffles. Marvin watched his mother lean back to dry her eyes. She took several deep breaths before folding her hands and leaning her head against them. Her lips moved in inaudible prayer. Colette and Marvin looked on silently, refusing to disturb this moment of reverence.

"You were just a kid, Marvin."

Colette's unexpected softheartedness shocked Marvin more than if she'd knocked him over. He met her gaze. It had softened from the state of derision to which he had become accustomed.

He searched her face for any sign of mockery but found none. She was in earnest.

He looked back to his mother, wishing to sit upon the chair next to her, wanting nothing more than to hold her, to apologize, to make everything his young self had done better.

The scene before him began to fade.

"Wait," called Marvin, reaching for his mother, but it was too late.

She was gone to the past forevermore.

Chapter Nine

As the room materialized around them, Marvin turned wildly. "Colette, I wasn't ready to go yet. Couldn't we go back?"

"No, we can't," said Colette. "That was the end of that one. I'm in less control this time." She paused. "If I was, I'd have given you more time."

Marvin looked at her wonderingly. "Really?"

She glanced at him, then nodded as she averted her eyes. "Really."

Marvin's heart dropped when he caught sight of the cross on the wall behind her. "Oh, no."

"You recognize where we are, then?"

"Of course." Marvin could never forget. They stood in the foyer of the chapel where the funeral services for Marvin's mother had been conducted. Everything was as Marvin remembered, from the unsuitably cheery bouquets of sunflowers at the front of the church to the kindly wife of the pastor who handed out programs for the day's event. The church even smelled the same, and Marvin's heart drooped beneath the same weight he had felt so many years before.

Colette and Marvin stood amid the mourners. Through the door at the front of the chapel, Marvin saw the casket which held his mother's body. As if driven by automation, he proceeded down the aisle, past the pews which were beginning to fill, and stepped up to the casket. He touched the mahogany surface lightly with his fingers, then took a deep breath and closed his eyes.

"She's probably the only person who loved me completely," Marvin said quietly.

"Of course she was," said Colette. "She's the only person who had no choice but to put up with your shit."

Marvin glared at Colette, gesturing to the scene before them. "A little respect for the dead, huh?"

She lifted her shoulders and let them drop. "I'm not disrespecting *her*."

He turned away.

"She did love you though," Colette said softly. "Probably more than you deserved."

Marvin bobbed his head, unable to argue the point.

The two were interrupted by a mourner who came to stand by the casket. Though it was functionally unnecessary, Marvin and Colette moved to allow him room. Upon catching sight of his face, Marvin jumped, though it was hardly surprising—only unsettling to see his own younger face.

"I was only nineteen when she died," said Marvin as he considered his younger self. His complexion was red, blotchy, and glistening with tears. The young Marvin wiped tears away with the back of his hand before laying a sunflower upon the casket. A young woman wearing a black dress stood beside him and, after doing the same, took his hand and resting her head upon his shoulder.

"Who's that?" asked Colette.

Present-Day Marvin said nothing and merely continued to look on, his brow wrinkling.

As the funeral wrapped up, mourners filtered out, but not Young Marvin and his female companion, not yet. As they stood there, another man approached.

"Mr. Hoeff?" he said. Both Young and Present-Day Marvin looked at him—Young with curiosity, Present-Day with an unreadable expression.

"That's me," said Young Marvin.

"I'm sorry for your loss. It's never easy to lose a parent." The man withdrew a business card from his pocket. "When you're ready, there are a few details of your mother's estate I need to discuss with you. Take your time."

Young Marvin frowned, looking at the card then back at the man.

When Young Marvin remained silent, the man spoke, "Nothing bad. Just things she'd want me to talk to you about. Okay? Don't worry about this." The man put his hand on his shoulder. "You've got enough on your mind today."

Young Marvin let out a breath, nodded, then mumbled, "Thanks."

"Of course." The man nodded acknowledgment to the woman beside Young Marvin before departing.

As he walked away, Young Marvin and the woman looked at one another, puzzled. Their focus returned to the casket, and the woman squeezed his arm.

"Ready?" she asked softly.

Young Marvin nodded, and they walked away hand in hand to take a seat in the front row.

"Do I have to stay for this?" Marvin asked.

Colette shook her head. "I think it's time for us to move on too."

In similar fashion to his young self, a stone-faced Marvin nodded acquiescence.

The scene before them changed to an office in which Young Marvin now sat in the middle of a row of chairs as lawyers and clerks passed him. By comparison, he looked like a lost little boy.

Into the room walked the same man from the day of the funeral. On the door was a plaque engraved with DAVID EVANS, ESQ.

"Mr. Hoeff, come on in," he said.

Young Marvin stood and walked in. Present-Day Marvin and Colette followed. As Young Marvin sat, his present-day counterpart and Colette stood along the side of the room where various framed diplomas and certifications were hung.

"Mr. Hoeff, thank you for coming in today," said the lawyer as he shook Marvin's hand.

"Sure," said Young Marvin.

The lawyer took a seat behind his desk. Young Marvin followed suit and sat, sinking into the squishy red chair.

"First of all, I want to reiterate how sorry I am for your loss," said the lawyer.

Marvin nodded in the practiced way the bereaved become accustomed to. "Thank you."

"Of course. The reason I've called you in today is that your mother entrusted care of her estate to me."

Young Marvin frowned. "Her estate?"

"Of course."

Young Marvin's confusion didn't abate, his eyebrows remaining furrowed.

The lawyer cleared his throat. "This may come as a nice surprise, then. Your mother has left you an inheritance."

"Oh," said Young Marvin, sounding neither pleased nor displeased.

The lawyer studied Marvin carefully. "It's rather sizeable."

Young Marvin frowned. "You mean . . . like a few thousand?"

Present-Day Marvin explained to Colette, "My car's suspension was out. When he said *sizeable*, that's the first thing that came to mind. It was such a piece of junk I was just hoping to replace it."

Colette nodded but didn't take her eyes off the scene. Present-Day Marvin looked on again as the lawyer spoke once more.

"It's actually around $8,000 from your mother's savings."

Young Marvin's eyes bugged out. "Holy shit."

The lawyer let out a short laugh before regaining his composure. "There's also the matter of her life insurance. She made sure I was aware of the details of it, but somehow I suspect you weren't."

"No," Young Marvin admitted.

"Given your reaction to the savings, I suppose I should brace you. Consider this statement doing so. With the accident rider added to the policy and given the cause of her death, you're entitled to $650,000."

Young Marvin turned white, unable to look more shocked if the lawyer had karate kicked him in the chest. "Holy shit," he repeated.

The lawyer sat quietly for a moment, watching with a good-natured smile on his face as he watched Marvin come to grips with the numbers. He seemed to intuit the correct moment to continue. "Now, son, this is a lot of money."

"You're telling me," Marvin choked.

The lawyer nodded. "For someone your age, this amount of money can be a blessing or a curse. I knew your mother well. She was a good woman. If I can help you avoid the latter, I wish to do so."

"Sure," said Young Marvin without argument.

"What I mean to say is, I strongly advise you see a financial advisor to manage it." The lawyer produced a business card from his desk drawer. "This is a friend of mine who can help."

"Okay."

The lawyer looked at him for another long moment before pushing the phone toward him. "Marvin, if you'll forgive my intrusion"—Marvin looked up curiously—"I'd like you to call him now."

Marvin frowned. "Why?"

"Because I remember being nineteen. I don't want to see you getting into trouble with what your mother intended as a gift." He gave the phone another gentle nudge. "Please."

"Oh, uh, okay." Young Marvin seemed flummoxed but obediently pulled the phone toward himself and began to dial.

Present-Day Marvin turned to Colette. "I had no idea what doors that money would open for me. I just thought about replacing my car and maybe buying a house. Maybe buying a car for my girlfriend or something. And I did. The financial advisor helped me invest most of it. But I did buy my first home with that money." He paused. "And my first investment property, a small four-unit complex."

"So that's where it all started," said Colette.

Marvin nodded.

Colette suggested, "Maybe the lawyer had a point about it being a blessing and a curse."

Marvin looked at Colette. "Please, I want to skip the rest."

"You can't walk away from this anymore, Marvin." The softness of her tone caught Marvin's attention more than any of her yelling had, and he almost didn't notice as his old self and the lawyer faded away.

When Marvin next looked at the desk, it was a different one—one he knew well. It was the very same office where he'd taken the call about Colette not so long ago.

Had that truly only been earlier that day? Marvin had passed through several lifetimes in the meantime. In different bodies, no less. The passing of fewer than 24 hours seemed impossible between then and this moment.

He and Colette now stood beside the desk of a Marvin who was older than in the last scene. This Marvin sat behind his desk, arms folded and brow furrowed. Standing before him was the same blonde woman who had accompanied him to the funeral. Her irritation mirrored Marvin's.

"Oh no," moaned Present-Day Marvin.

The blonde woman brushed her hair over her shoulder and sighed heavily. She looked away from Young Marvin to a point on the wall and shook her head, her jaw set. She looked back to her companion, her eyes fierce. "You've changed."

"*Linda*," said Young Marvin with incredulity. "This is who I am. I give you everything you want." He held out his arms. "What more can I do?"

"You haven't been home before dark for days. You could have someone do this work for you."

"Damn it, Linda. I just bought this new property. I have to save where I can. Why don't you get that?"

Linda glared at him. "You're selfish." When Marvin looked affronted, she doubled down. "Selfish. You don't truly care about anyone but yourself. It's all about *you*."

"How can you possibly say that? I make a good living. I don't see you complaining about the car, the clothing. The jewelry, every holiday!"

"I want more than that," interrupted Linda.

Young Marvin leaned forward, his eyes gleaming. "*Well*," he spat, "Who's selfish now, then? I've spent a small fortune trying to keep you happy, and you say you want *more*?"

Linda closed her eyes, shaking her head once more, then spoke more quietly. "That's not what I mean."

"Then what do you mean?"

When she opened her eyes again, they glistened with tears. "I need more than just things. I want a family. Kids. Cats. A dog, maybe. A picket fence. The whole nine yards. I want the messiness of a beautiful life with you, full of love."

Young Marvin looked genuinely perplexed. "Don't you like the life we have now? We can go anywhere. We can do anything. Kids and pets, they'd ruin all that." It was his turn to shake his head and sigh. "Why can't *I* just be enough for you?"

Linda smiled sadly, lifted a shoulder and dropped it. "I don't even have you."

"What do you mean?"

"You're never home."

"But—"

"No." She wiped away a tear. "All the money in the world doesn't mean anything if there's no actual *future* to look forward to."

Marvin stared at Linda for a long moment, his face cycling through anger, shock, dismay, despair, then outrage.

"Fine. Fine. Throw this all away, then." He rubbed his temples before looking at her again. His hand thumped the desk, disturbing a pen sitting upon it. "Leave, then, if I'm not enough for you."

Linda tilted her head to the side, looking upon Young Marvin. Her lips parted a moment before she spoke quietly. "I loved you, Marvin. I hope you know that."

Young Marvin looked at her, his eyes blank, empty. He said nothing, and Linda turned and left, slamming the door behind her.

Present-Day Marvin spoke quietly. "Can we please leave?" He turned to see Colette watching him. "Please, I don't want to be here anymore."

The scene before them carried on in a much quieter fashion as Young Marvin sat at his chair and drank a small bottle of whiskey which had evidently been kept in his desk drawer.

"This is the day Linda saw you for who you really were. The only thing you really cared about."

"I loved her," said Marvin. "It . . ." He trailed off, then sighed. "Nothing was the same without her."

"Why didn't you want to, you know, have the kids and the pets and stuff?"

Marvin chuckled without humor. "I still don't like kids. Or pets. But maybe I would have liked them with her. I just knew what it was to be poor, invisible, powerless, and unimportant. I didn't want to be just another Joe Schmoe with a mortgage and an HOA breathing down his neck. It seemed like that's what she wanted. I wanted . . ." He sighed. "I don't know what I wanted."

"Did you ever find out?"

Marvin looked at Colette with surprise, having never considered that question until now. He looked at his young self for a long moment before answering. "I don't know."

"It's time we move on to the, shall we say, Ghost of Marvin Present."

Marvin watched his younger self massage his forehead in despair for a moment before agreeing.

Chapter Ten

Marvin briefly mistook the next apartment for Colette's, being that it was undoubtedly a unit in the Riverbrook complex. Each of its one-bedroom apartments had an identical layout. However, as his eyes adjusted, Marvin realized it couldn't be Colette's. The furniture was different. Still sparse, but not quite as sad as hers had been. The darkness outside indicated nighttime.

Nighttime. Present day. This was as present as it got. Marvin was almost back to the real world, and relief accompanied this realization.

"Whose apartment is this?" asked Marvin, but as if to answer his question, Abhi walked out of his bedroom.

Marvin jumped, momentarily flummoxed by being in Abhi's space uninvited. *I'm not really here*, he reminded himself. To prove his point, Abhi's eyes never flicked in his direction, no shouting match ensued, nothing which would have happened had Marvin really materialized in Abhi's apartment after the day's conflict. Abhi looked haggard as he walked to the kitchen. A woman soon joined Abhi in the kitchen. She rested her back against the counter as she watched her counterpart study bottles of liquor before settling on a bottle of whiskey. He grabbed a glass and placed a few ice cubes in it.

"I must find a new job," said Abhi. He poured rum over the ice and took a sip.

His female companion looked at him sadly. "It's too much."

Abhi looked at her. "Can you believe his first concern was the money? After seeing . . . *that*."

"He's miserable."

Abhi nodded. "Yes."

"No, I mean it, Abhi. He has nothing but his money. It's all that matters to him. It's sad, isn't it?"

Abhi furrowed his brow. "I thought there was more to him, possibly."

"You can't let it get to you, Abhi. You're a good man." She sighed. "Not everyone is."

"He truly is as bad as they say he is."

"Worse," the woman offered with a grin, but it wasn't returned.

"I thought I could help."

"Of course you did. Because you're a good man," the woman reiterated. "But you can't force someone to change. You did your best."

Instead, Abhi took another sip of his drink. "Tomorrow, I will start looking for another job."

"Good."

"And perhaps I'll tell the bastard to—" Abhi finished his sentence in a foreign language and a universally understood gesture.

The woman snorted with laughter. "*Good.* That's more like it. I honestly don't know how you've worked for him this long."

"No rent," said Abhi simply. "For this economy, it has been a decent job."

"Pour me some for me, too, will you? Then we can search listings together in bed." The woman winked and went back to the other room. Abhi poured a drink for her, this time with a cola mixed in, and brought it with him and shut the door.

Colette looked at Marvin, whose shoulders had drooped.

"What?" he asked.

"What do you think?"

Marvin turned away, studying the bare walls of Abhi's apartment. "I thought he had more respect for me."

"What made you think that?"

Marvin ignored the implied insult. "He's been my most reliable property manager. The one who's stayed longest, anyway. And he's always so polite."

"Because he's a polite person, not because you deserve politeness."

Marvin clenched his jaw in annoyance.

Colette continued, "Sounds like money—power—doesn't buy respect."

Marvin sighed. "Then what does?"

Colette smiled. "Time for the next."

The new scene which took shape was far less familiar to Marvin. It certainly wasn't a unit at Riverbrook. He and Colette stood at the center of the room where golden sunlight illuminated mismatched furniture and a mess of children's toys. A large orange cat snoozed upon a threadbare cat tower in the corner of the room.

Marvin cringed, associating such sights with colored-on walls, scratched-up carpets, and pissed-on everything. He looked beyond the furnishings and tried to identify where they were. Then, finally, it clicked.

"Grove Street," he said.

Colette nodded. "Yes, the home of Matthew and Sara Mosely."

Marvin narrowed his eyes, trying to place the name Mosely. He had to have met them. Was Grove Street the one he'd tried outsourcing? He racked his brain and came up with nothing. "I don't remember them."

"You'll see." Colette held up a finger to indicate he should wait.

A mewling sound echoed from the next room. A sleepy-eyed woman with a mussed ponytail emerged, shushing a fussy baby whose tiny head was covered in delicate blond curls. Following close behind was a messy-haired toddler who cuddled a stuffed lion to her chest. Marvin was able to step out of the way this time and avoid the discomfort of being walked through by the trio.

"This is Sara Mosely," Colette explained.

Sara and the infant sat on the couch, then she looked to the toddler. "Zoey, if you bring me a book, I'll read to you while Riley nurses."

"Okay, Mama," said the toddler.

While she bobbed off to grab a book from an ill-organized shelf, Sara latched the baby to nurse. When the little girl returned, Sara took the book and helped her up to the couch. Zoey snuggled against her mother's side to see the book's illustrations.

Marvin looked upon the idyllic scene with an urge to check his watch. "Is this it?" he asked.

"Hush."

Marvin shrugged. "I mean . . ." Silenced by another look from Colette, he sighed. "Fine."

Sara finished the book about several differently colored fish, then began again at the toddler's insistence. Marvin's mind wandered as he considered the property. A thought struck him, and he frowned. "This is just a one-bedroom. Shouldn't they have something bigger with two kids?"

"Can't afford it," said Colette.

Marvin scoffed. "Maybe they shouldn't have had those kids, then."

A sharp smack met the back of Marvin's head. He yelped. "What the hell was that for?"

"Stop being an asshole."

He pointed. "The children."

"They can't hear me. Shut up and watch."

Marvin reluctantly acquiesced, closing his mouth and pantomiming zipping it shut.

The doorbell rang. Sara looked up at the door, then down at the suckling infant, frazzled for a moment before a man—Matthew, Marvin gathered—emerged from the hallway.

"Sit," he said with a smile as he fastened the top button of his shirt, "I've got it."

Sara settled back into the couch gratefully and resumed reading a book to the little girl pulling at her arm to complain about the delay.

Matthew walked to the door and opened it to reveal a young woman who spoke in an apologetic flurry. "I'm so sorry, I know it's early and you guys are probably busy, but I didn't know where else to go."

"Hey, it's okay," said Matthew. "What's up?"

"Oh, the babysitter canceled—stomach flu or something—and my husband is in a bad way today. I'm supposed to go in for an appointment this morning and I don't know what to do with Isla. I mean, I guess she could play on my phone, but some of the appointment is kind of sensitive and . . ."

Marvin looked on and saw a little girl standing beside her mother.

Sara spoke from the couch. "Jess, it's okay. Isla can totally hang out this morning."

Jess's whole posture softened. "Oh, thank you so much."

"It's nothing, really," said Sara. As if to underscore the point, the little girl beside Sara bounded to the door and peered out at the playmate. Sara spoke again, saying, "Zoey, why don't you show Isla where the books are? We can read a little more, then have breakfast."

Isla looked at her mother, who kneeled and gave her a hug, murmuring something into her ear.

"Love you too, Mommy," said Isla, who walked into the house, led away by her little counterpart.

As the conversation regarding choosing books and what the kids might have for breakfast ensued, Colette said, "That's Jessica Hutchinson. She's in the process of trying to leave her abusive husband, but she hasn't told anyone."

Marvin raised an eyebrow. "And?"

"*And*," Colette went on, "she and Isla have no one right now, except for the Moselys. They're always around to help. Always. And she's one of many."

"Swell for them."

There was a pause before Colette said, "Marvin, you're a smart guy."

"You make that sound like an insult."

"You're a smart guy, and you haven't pieced anything together about them, have you?"

"What's to piece?"

Colette sighed. "They're not exactly well-off. They've got a one-bedroom apartment with four people in it."

"Think that's more than the fire code allows."

"Good God *Almighty*. Not the *point*. Jesus *Christ*." Colette massaged her eyebrows for a moment. "This is all they can afford. Sara cries every night, worried about how they'll feed the kids, pay the rent, everything. Their kids know none of it, just their parents' love. And that? That's what they offer to everyone. *Love*. In spite of their own poverty, they give everything they can."

"Swell."

"They give their time, their food, their love, everything they can," reiterated Colette.

Repulsed by the schmaltz, Marvin sighed and gave Colette a thumbs-up. "Great."

"In return," Colette continued, "let me show you something."

Colette withdrew something resembling a cell phone from a pocket in her dress and pointed it toward the family. The screen rendered them in a way reminiscent of heat-detection technology. It wasn't heat detection, though. They had transformed, taking on a kind of iridescence. Marvin looked upon the family once more, momentarily slack-jawed.

"They're beautiful," he whispered.

"Mmhmm. Now take a look at yourself." Colette turned the screen toward Marvin.

Instead of a glowing light from within, he saw a creature composed of a black, tarry substance. He held out his hand, turning it over before his eyes. Marvin gasped. "The fuck?"

"Do you see what I see, Marvin?"

"What did you do to me?" he squealed.

"Oh, Marv, don't you see? You've done this to yourself, you selfish bastard. You've blackened your soul, leaned into the awfulness therein, and well, that's all that's left."

Marvin looked horrified between himself and the family. Where they looked to be ethereal beings, his appearance was that of a swamp-dweller.

"They have nothing material-wise. In your eyes, they are nothing. But the truth is, you have made yourself nothing by being so selfish and they, well, look at them. Aren't they glorious?"

Marvin was struck dumb for the first time in a long time. What struck him even more was the look on Colette's face, one of deep thought. Was it possible that she looked nervous?

"Why the long face?" asked Marvin. "I thought you'd be smug."

She looked at him for a long time, longer than he was prepared for. "I have to show you something else."

She turned the screen on herself.

Chapter Eleven

"I'm more like you than them," said Colette softly.

Marvin took the device from her and ran it along Colette's arm. He had the fleeting urge to gloat, followed by a flicker of something like sympathy before his mind finally settled upon anger. His jaw stiffened. "So what gives you the right to lead me around like this, to point out all my flaws?"

Colette withdrew her arm and snatched the device back from Marvin. Isla ran past, the device passing unresistingly through her.

"You think this is all just for fun?" asked Colette.

"What did I do to make you hate me so much?" demanded Marvin. "As bad a person as I may be, I can't imagine doing this to someone."

Colette closed her eyes, eyebrows knitted. The device was folded safely into her arms.

"I have a right to know," Marvin continued, "Considering what you've put me through this evening."

Colette looked at him. Her eyes were wet, and not from the remnants of her bath water. The sight shocked him as much as any other this evening. "You're right, Marvin," she said with a sniff. "I do kind of hate you. But this is just as much for me as it is for you." Her eyes softened as she looked at him. "If I can change you, long shot though it may be, I get a certain kind of escape as well."

"From what?"

She gestured to the black metal cuff around her ankle. "Haven't you wondered what this was for?"

"I haven't had much time to," he confessed. "What kind of escape do you get?"

She stood, seeming to contemplate this question for a moment. She looked back toward the family. The mother was now negotiating a truce between two children who wanted the same book as the father took his squalling infant.

"I have to take you somewhere else."

"I want an answer," demanded Marvin.

Before he could argue the point further, everything went dark again.

This time, however, it remained dark until there was a soft *ffwwtt* sound of what Marvin soon realized was a match. Colette's face swam before him once more, lit by the flame.

"Do you know where you are now, Marvin?" she asked.

"No," he admitted.

"You're in the dark."

Marvin frowned and resisted the impulse to say, *Yes, thank you, I could tell that much.*

"Do you happen to know why that's significant?" continued Colette.

He shook his head. "Not even a little."

"Because after all your life, after everything you've done, *this* is what you have to look forward to."

Marvin looked at his surroundings—or tried to. Nothing was visible aside from Colette.

"*This*, Marv. This is what you have to come home to after your life is over. This. Nothingness. This abyss. Just imagine." She paused, studying him, before blowing out the flame.

Darkness overtook Marvin entirely, a pitch blackness far beyond anything he had ever experienced. Opening and closing his eyes changed nothing about his perception.

"Imagine living in this darkness with nothing but yourself, your thoughts, your memories to accompany you."

As if the darkness wasn't unsettling enough, the sensation of Marvin's body melted away.

"Woah, what . . . ?"

How he could still speak, he wasn't sure, but all other bodily sensations had gone. He couldn't feel his skin, couldn't touch one hand to the other, he had nothing. Even the unsettling sensation of blinking was gone; for as best he could tell, he had no eyes or accompanying lids.

He was, to the best of his knowledge, a floating brain.

Images of the evening ran through his mind of all the awful things he had done, all the pain he had caused.

Zeus as he had been, followed by a glimpse of the heartbroken little boy who didn't know what had happened to his cat. The boy's mother rubbed his back as he colored pictures of the cat to add to a missing poster, a poster which would do nothing because of what Marvin had done. His cat would never come home. Marvin witnessed the boy, lying in bed, fuming at the realization that it wasn't something which had simply happened to his cat, but which had been done to him. A seed of bitterness grew within the young boy, something which, left unchecked, would blossom and spread its seeds in others.

Poor Abhi, lying restlessly in bed beside his snoozing bed companion, troubled by Marvin's despicable nature. He said prayers for Colette's soul—and some for his own, wondering how to redeem himself from his complicity in Marvin's actions, despite his best attempts to help.

A view of Colette's apartment before she committed suicide, wherein she sat at the table reading the late notice for rent, along with a lease renewal indicating that if she wanted to stay in the apartment, she owed an extra $150 a month and another $500 to add to the security deposit. He watched her pallid face, dry and tearless, fill with resignation of what she would do to avoid homelessness.

Misery, despair, depression, anger, mistreatment abounded. The court, indifferent to his own sufferings, the same way he had ignored those of the people around him. A glimpse of his worst unit and the mold festering within, another with a cockroach issue the tenants hadn't had the courage to bring to him yet. The misery of everything, along with the misery of being neglected and left alone.

"This is awful," said Marvin, able to do nothing to assuage his anxiety over the images he saw. Another match was struck, illuminating Colette's face, and Marvin's bodily sensations returned. He touched his arms, grateful for the brief lessening of his torment, but still perturbed.

"It's what you've built over a lifetime of shitty misdeeds. This is what you've earned, Marvin, and you have no one to blame but yourself for the hell you've created." She bit her lip. "But I was about to go to a similar place."

Marvin frowned, searching her face for any sign of irony, but found none. "For what?"

"I haven't lived a spotless life myself, and killing myself was the—pardon the pun—final nail in the coffin. When I was dying, I reached out toward the light, but it... uh, rejected me." She coughed. "I lived a self-centered life like you, just different. I didn't do the things you do, but I had my own trouble."

"I'll say," said Marvin, softer than he might have before.

Colette's eyes narrowed, but capitulation lingered upon her face as well. "I was given a chance to cleanse myself, you could say. By changing you. Something rescued me and gave me gave me an offer. That's not to say I didn't find a certain *je ne sais quoi* in torturing you, considering the stupid rent increase and *especially* when I learned all the horrid things you'd done to other people. But maybe there's more to it than that. I mean, do you feel anything for these people? Do you feel anything for me?"

Marvin paused, considering Colette for a moment. "Why did you kill yourself?"

"Do you really want to know?"

"Yes."

"Well, it was a lot of things. It all just built up to the point where it felt like nothing mattered anymore—least of all me. I just wanted out."

"You said I fucked up your life."

Colette nodded, slowly meeting his gaze. "The final straw was that notice I got about rent increasing."

Marvin looked away and mumbled something about market value.

"What about people value? I mean, did you really need that extra money? Was it hurting you not to have it?"

"Well, no."

"That's why I've hated you so much. The extra $150 a month hardly affected you, but it was the final straw for me." She swallowed, face hardening. "Do you get that?"

Marvin sat with the idea, casting his mind back to the time before his mother's death, when he had a shitty car and a shitty apartment and was barely making ends meet. Dredging up what otherwise might have seemed an eternity ago made it feel much more recent. More relevant.

"I know what it's like to feel like you don't matter. I've spent my life trying to make sure that never happens again."

"And you've hurt so many people in the process," Colette said.

Marvin paused, taking a deep breath, and slowly, finally, nodded. *Pain begets pain.* And he had caused a lot of it.

"And your soul is hideous because of it," she added.

"So what do I do, then?" he asked.

Colette tucked her hair behind her ear. "I can't change what I did in life. I gave in, gave up. Maybe I could have handled it, maybe I would have been homeless. It doesn't matter much now. But I can help you. Because maybe what really matters—what really makes someone matter—is who they are in relation to others. It's not about what you have, it's about how you make those around you feel. I failed that. So have you. But you've still got a chance."

Marvin mentally rehearsed everything he had just witnessed, everything he had experienced, from revisiting his childhood and college days, to the death of his dear, sweet mother who had tried so hard. He remembered Linda, who had been so disappointed to find out who he was deep down inside. Then he considered the disturbing image of his dark inner self compared to the brilliant glow of the good, charitable Mosely family.

A strange feeling overcame him, one he had never experienced in this context before. It was usually reserved for when his stock portfolio dipped in value or when he lost a bet.

Shame. He felt shame.

"And if you still have a chance, then so do I," Colette said softly.

The abyssal darkness was somehow the worst torment yet. He wasn't sure whether Colette knew this, nor could he find it within himself to admit so out loud. He recognized his own great and negative impact on the world. Maybe he did have a responsibility to rectify it, especially if he could save more than one soul in the process.

As he thought about the young boy whose heart was filled with bitterness because of his lost best friend, a panic rose within Marvin's heart.

"I'm just a bad person," said Marvin. "How do I change that?"

"Now you're asking the right questions," Colette said, a genuine smile breaking over her face. "Finally."

"Really, though, how does someone like me change who they are?" He gestured from his head to his feet. "How do I change this? I'm no Ebenezer Scrooge. I'm not..." He sighed. "I don't have a heart of gold."

Colette laughed. "No, you don't."

"I'm serious," said Marvin, dropping his hands to his side helplessly.

"I can help you."

Marvin frowned. "Does it have to be you?"

Colette nodded. "Yes."

"Really, though, I can't do more of this." He gestured around himself. "I can't."

"You don't have to, Marvin. I said I'll help you, and I will."

"But how?" Marvin's mind went immediately to multiple torture chambers and more of the same he had experienced this evening.

Colette considered him for a moment. "Do you remember the story of Pinocchio?"

Marvin frowned. "I guess?"

"What about his cricket conscience thing?"

Marvin nodded, not liking where this was going.

"I'll be your cricket," said Colette.

"Oh, I don't know . . ." Marvin trailed off, trying to think of some excuse. Could he have Colette hanging around him all the time? "Like forever?"

"Unless you think you can do it yourself," said Colette with an eyebrow arched. When Marvin further hesitated, she blew out the flame again. Darkness enveloped him once more.

Darkness forever?

"How do I know you're telling the truth?" asked Marvin to the blackness surrounding him.

"Not sure how else to prove it," came Colette's voice.

This was just intolerable. As the sensation of his body dissolved once more, he said, "Okay. Okay."

A soft *fwwt*, and the light returned, illuminating a smile on Colette's face.

"I don't want to be stuck with you any more than you want to be stuck with me," admitted Colette. "But maybe we deserve each other."

"I can't do anymore reformations. No more Zeus. No more rotten food. No more spiders. No more..." *Mom* is the word he choked on, then swallowed back more tears. "No more of this darkness."

"You don't have to, Marvin. I said I'll help you, and I will."

Chapter Twelve

I need a fucking aspirin, thought Marvin with a sigh. *Or a priest.*

His limbs were tired, heavy, and reluctant to be moved, like he would imagine being drugged would feel. With great effort, Marvin lolled his head from one side to the other and drew a deep breath. His head throbbed as he moved to sit up, cradling his head in his hands. When he had gone to bed the night before, it seemed the following day would be a long one. It had only gotten longer.

Nonetheless, he was back.

He was solid again: his body, his eyes, his heart, and his lungs. And light surrounded him. All of it had returned. His hands moved over his own soft sheets on his own bed in his own room. No rats, no spiders, no beetles, no pests of any kind.

If he wasn't delusional, he was home once more. Granted, he had been wrong before, but perhaps the worst really was over.

Or...

Could it be that he'd only had a very long, very terrible, very vivid dream? He thought about the conversation he seemed to have just had with Colette. Maybe it was a fever dream, the result of a bit of trauma from seeing Colette's death scene. Only a crisis of conscience mixed with a little indigestion.

Food poisoning, more like.

It had all been so much. But had any of it been real? Marvin was beginning to doubt himself when he heard a familiar voice.

"I mean it."

Marvin looked up, and, sure enough, though he was in his own bedroom once more, Colette was still there, sitting upon his chair. The sewery smell which had accompanied her appearance the night before reached his nose.

Marvin looked around himself at his own room, then sat up in bed. "Am I really home?" he asked. In grasping for any foothold upon reality, talking to the phantom seemed unfortunately to be his best choice.

Colette nodded. "And I really will help you."

The courtroom. Zeus. The exploding money. The house which had turned against him. Himself as a boy and his mother, alive, once more. Linda. The lawyer who had worked to change his life for . . . the better? He had to wonder now. But it all seemed to have been real.

Even that dark, dark future.

Marvin looked Colette over from the top of her wet hair down past her sundress to her shoeless feet. All of it had been real.

But that meant the hope for change was, too.

"Does the smell have to stay?" Marvin asked.

Colette shook her head. "No."

As quickly as it had reappeared, it faded. Why had it been there in the first place? *Probably to annoy me.* He searched Colette's face uncertainly. It held an undeniable softness it hadn't before.

He recalled the conversation surrounding the cricket-conscience deal. "How can you help me?"

Colette crossed her legs and leaned back against the chair. "Like I said, you aren't a good guy deep down inside. Maybe I'm not so good myself. Maybe that's why I'm the one who can help you."

"What do you mean?"

"The only way I can imagine helping you be a better guy is by, well, forcing your hand." Her eyes gleamed unsettlingly as she said this.

"I don't like the sound of that," said Marvin.

Colette smiled in response. She had a bit of the Cheshire cat quality from before, but less menacing. "Relax. It's not so bad."

"Do I have to do more of"—Marvin jerked a thumb backward as if to indicate what had happened the previous night—"that?"

"Be a good boy and you won't," she said.

Marvin groaned. Colette giggled, then sighed, looking at him more seriously. "I said I would help you. I meant it. But that means you're never getting rid of me."

Marvin paused, searching her face for any sign she wasn't entirely in earnest. "Never?"

She shook her head. "Never. If you can't be trusted to make good decisions on your own, I'll hold your hand like a little toddler and help you."

Marvin slumped. "Frankly, that sounds unpleasant. No offense."

She shrugged. "It might be the only way to save both of us."

"So tell me what that means, then."

"Pretty much, I'll help you do the right things. I'll be happy to give you advice. No one will see me but you. And if you don't make the right choices, well . . ."

At once, Colette transformed into something like a werewolf, leaping upon Marvin and pinning him quite unsensually to his bed. "I'll be waiting."

A feminine shriek gurgled from Marvin's throat, and Colette turned back into her normal form—the one Marvin was most well-acquainted with, anyway. She stood beside his bed like a nurse checking on a patient.

Marvin rested a hand upon his chest and felt his heartbeat slow again. "You're going to force me to be good."

Colette nodded in agreement. "I'm going to force you to be good."

Marvin settled back against the headboard, recalling the blackness beneath his skin at the Mosely's home, how he had recoiled at the sight of his internal hideousness—and that awful, awful darkness. Was there no alternative?

"Maybe it's not even about you or me anyway," said Colette. "But the fact that the people around you deserve better. They deserve to be given a shit about. They deserve a better life—and death—than both of us."

There had to be another way. He didn't want that future, but he didn't want to be pummeled in the present, either.

"But what about shitty tenants?" Marvin argued. "And what about your unit? There really is water damage, plus biohazard cleanup and all the rest." Without getting compensation from Mr. Finch, the financial damage threw Marvin into a pit of despair.

She paused for a moment before haltingly adding, "You're not wrong."

Marvin raised an eyebrow.

"But what if I can work for you in more than one way?" she continued. "I can help you be a good person, but I can also help protect you from others. Maybe you get something good out of the deal after all. Maybe I can be your conscience but also your guardian angel, a little bit."

"Angel?" scoffed Marvin. "More like a demon."

Colette smiled, hardly looking offended by the comparison. "But really. Think about it."

Maybe.

Weren't there costs and benefits to every transaction? Colette's meddling would undoubtedly cost him. On the other hand, he would gain a secret weapon to prevent himself from being victimized. It didn't sound entirely pleasant, but when he considered that awful darkness, it also seemed like hardly a choice.

"Okay. Let's do this." He sighed and rubbed his face. "So what now, then? What am I doing on my first day of being a bleeding heart?"

"Oh, now, that's a bit dramatic." Colette waved away the complaint.

"I feel a bit like I've been castrated."

"You poor eunuch."

"I'm serious." He raised his eyebrows. "I don't know how to do this."

"You won't have to do this alone, remember? I'll follow you to the end of your life, until your last dying breath."

Marvin's expression darkened. "That's not nearly as comforting as I think you think it is."

Colette responded with a giggle. "Guardian angel, remember?"

Marvin turned and looked at his bedside table. His alarm clock glowed 9:07 AM. Morning had arrived, and it was already far past time for Marvin to begin the first day of his gelded life.

Part of him wished Colette had just thrown him off the balcony to meet his fate. It would have been far simpler.

Though he had showered the night before, Marvin felt the distinct need for another. It was as though he had lived several lifetimes between then and now. He had even swapped species, for Christ's sake, and he could do with some freshening up. He sullenly stepped into the shower, remembering how much simpler things had seemed the night before. But when he looked at his skin, he saw only the vision of the blackness underneath. Like a fetid swamp. At the memory, he doused his washcloth in body wash and scrubbed his body, trying to slough away the filth. He wasn't sure he would ever feel clean again, not after having seen what lay beneath.

But Colette, his bizarre watershed moment in the form of a deranged psychopath, was certain he could change. And he was certain she was annoying enough to do, well, something.

He rinsed off the soap, then paused for a moment before repeating the whole routine. By the time he rinsed off the soap, his skin was red and raw, but at least a bit cleaner. He turned off the water. Steam rose from his skin like from a boiled lobster. He grabbed a towel, then dried himself off before exiting the shower.

He stood before the mirror and wiped away the fog with a washcloth to gaze upon his reflection.

"You're a changed man, Marvin," he said to himself. "Whether you like it or not."

A disembodied finger drew a smiley face on the unwiped edge of the mirror. Marvin closed his eyes against the irritation and turned around, refusing to acknowledge the presence until he reached his bedroom. He called out into the ether, "At least give me a little privacy while I'm getting dressed, will you?"

There was no response. Just in case, Marvin dressed with the modesty usually reserved for a gym locker room. Even though she had likely seen everything the night before, and even though she probably would forevermore. They would become quite intimate with time, he realized.

Maybe I should *call a priest*, thought Marvin, but he didn't need Colette's protestation to recognize the futility of this action. He was pretty sure Colette was his to keep.

But, he had to recall, it had been his choice.

Still, he had sacrificed his old self to not only become better, but also to be a kind of plaything for her. He recalled the Colette-werewolf from that morning. Maybe reforming him was part of her reforming herself, but there was an undeniable level of enjoyment she got out of it. Like Zeus when he'd been a mouse.

At least she was leaving him alone for now. He pulled up his underwear and pants, then put on an undershirt and a button-down shirt. None of it felt right anymore. *Probably the missing balls*, he thought disdainfully, then sighed. He had an opportunity to change. He was able to avoid the fate that had been lain for him. That was a good thing, right?

Blessing though it might be, his new obligation do something about it annoyed him almost as much as the smiley face on the mirror. As he fastened the last button on his shirt, a slow-building panic set in. What was he supposed to do now? Was he supposed to start buying cardigans and playing with puppets? *Come sit on my knee, kiddo, I like you just the way you are.*

Nope, not that. Colette could never persuade him to go that far. But *what*, then? Who would Marvin Hoeff become?

He reflected on the night prior. What needled him most was the vision of Zeus's former owner and the seed of bitterness that had been planted within his heart. A similar seed, he realized, to the one planted by his own father's neglect.

Marvin knew exactly where his new life should begin.

Chapter Thirteen

One whiff of a trip to the animal shelter sent Colette scrambling aboard Marvin's train of thought. The pair now sat in the shelter's meet and greet room, a fluffy gray kitten upon Marvin's lap. The tiny thing, no larger than a soda can, had a pink nose and markings like white socks on three of four of his tiny feet. None of these feet were visible at present as the kitten was folded into a loaf, rumbling with appreciation for the warm lap.

"Is this one good enough?" Marvin asked.

"What do you mean? He's *adorable*," fussed Colette, wiggling her fingers in front of the kitten's face. "I wish I could pet him."

"Great." Marvin stood and left the small room, then walked with the kitten to the nearby desk where a shelter worker sat. "We'll take him."

The shelter worker turned around, her pleasant face crossed with a slight frown.

"Who's we?" giggled Colette in Marvin's ear.

He waved a hand as though to wave away a persistent fly.

The shelter worker continued unperturbed. "Well, I'm glad to hear it. His littermates were adopted out yesterday and he's been all alone."

"Well, he won't be anymore," said Marvin with a reluctant sigh, rubbing the fur behind the kitten's ears. "I've got a boy who will really love him."

The woman beamed. "That's wonderful."

When filling out the paperwork for the kitten, the shelter worker fawned over what a good father he must be. Marvin remained quiet. He wasn't used to being the recipient of such chatter, but it wasn't entirely unpleasant. He even found himself joining in the excitement when he noticed the way her eyes glimmered as she spoke about benign issues like the boy's favorite color—Marvin decided it was blue—to choose a collar he'd like most. She found such joy in a little boy's happiness, a boy she had no connection to. What must that be like?

With all the paperwork completed, Marvin and Colette ventured to the home of the former owner of Zeus. The family had since bought a house on the other side of town which was about a thirty-minute drive. Marvin drummed his fingers to the beat of a song on the radio along the way. He exited the freeway, humming as he entered the neighborhood.

"This the place?" asked Marvin, referring to a gray house on the south side of Maple Avenue.

"Yep, 6799 Maple Avenue," came Colette's voice. "That's the one."

Who needs GPS when you've got a phantom?

He pulled into the driveway alongside a silver minivan, killed the engine, then got out and walked to the door, his heart racing as he knocked.

After a momentary wait, a pretty, dark-haired woman answered the door. The boy's mother, Marvin assumed.

"Can I help you?"

Marvin's next words came out in a deluge before he lost his nerve. "Hi. I don't know if you remember me. I own the building you lived in when you had your cat, Zeus. This little guy needs a home, and I heard your boy lost his cat. I don't know why I'm here, really, I just . . ."

The mother's mouth dropped open, and she paused for a moment, eyebrows knitted in confusion as she studied Marvin.

"Is this weird?" asked Marvin.

The woman smiled. "No. No, it's okay." She let out a short laugh. "I remember you."

Marvin said nothing as he stood holding the cat. The woman glanced between the mismatched pair. Her recollection didn't seem positive. She narrowed her eyes. "Really? With the cat?"

Marvin nodded. "I-I found him, someone abandoned him in one of my units, and I remembered Zeus. But if you don't want him, it's—"

"No really," she cut in, laughing a little. "That. . . is unexpectedly kind of you. I mean, really, this is so unexpected, but well..." She trailed off, looking behind herself, then called out, "Archer, there's someone at the door for you."

Thudding footsteps followed and the light-haired, brokenhearted boy from Marvin's visions the night before appeared. He looked with confusion from Marvin to the cat.

"I don't know if you remember him," the mother said, "But this is the guy who owned our last apartment."

The boy frowned, shaking his head.

His mother continued, "He heard about Zeus, and how sad you were. He said he found this cat and thought of you."

The boy glowered a little at the mention of his old cat, but his expression relaxed when he eyed the kitten in Marvin's arms. The kitten squirmed within his grip and Marvin held tighter, worried he would get hurt if he leaped from this height.

"Why?"

Marvin looked at the boy and swallowed hard. *Because I killed Zeus*, thought Marvin, *because it's my fault*. Instead, he sighed and said, "Because this guy's pretty lonely. Someone left him behind." Marvin looked from the cat to Archer, unsure what to say to wipe the well-deserved skepticism from the boy's face.

Colette whispered in his ear, making Marvin jump. "He deserves to know there's good in the world, not just the bad."

Marvin recovered, swallowed, then said, "Maybe you both deserve to know there's good people in the world. And not just bad ones."

The mother rubbed her son's shoulder with great appreciation on her face. His expression softened as well.

"Do you mean it?" he asked quietly.

Marvin nodded. "Really. He needs a home."

"And you need a cat," whispered Colette.

"And you need a cat," said Marvin, mouth twisting because it seemed like such a cheesy thing to say.

Archer frowned, this time less in skepticism and more in wonder, then met Marvin's eye. "Thank you," he said, and reached out for the kitten.

"Of course," said Marvin.

The absence of the kitten's pleasant, innocent warmth was unexpectedly bittersweet for Marvin. All bitterness evaporated, however, when Marvin caught sight of the boy's face as he met his new cat for the first time. Archer's eyes relaxed, a brightness coming to them. His soft grin turned into a big, toothy smile when the cat swatted at his nose. All misgivings seemed to fall away as he bonded with the kitten. His young face looked less wary, more open.

Maybe the new kitten couldn't take the place of his old friend but could help heal the wound Marvin had caused. Might Marvin's unification of the two help heal Archer's distrust of the world at large? Marvin could only hope so.

"What's his name?" asked Archer, scratching his cat's belly.

"He doesn't have one yet," said Marvin.

"Thor," supplied Colette.

"What about Thor?" asked the mother.

Marvin resisted the urge to look at Colette. *Could she hear her?* "Or Loki."

The mother laughed. "The God of mischief. Perfect."

"Loki," repeated Archer, who then held the cat up in front of him. "I like it." He tucked the kitten close to his chest and looked at Marvin again. "You mean it? I can really keep him?"

Marvin nodded. "Of course." He coughed. "You and Loki have a good time." He put two fingers to his temple then saluted before turning to leave.

"Wait," said the boy.

Marvin turned around, fearing the boy had sussed out exactly why he'd come. He anticipated accusations, threats, and questions. Instead, the little boy dashed to him, holding the kitten under one arm, and wrapped him in a hug. Marvin started, then softened, returning the embrace with an awkward pat on the boy's back. The little cat mewed, perhaps worried about being squished.

"Sure thing, kid," said Marvin.

The boy let go and returned to his mother, who wrapped an arm around his shoulder.

"This was a really kind thing for you to do," she said. "Thank you."

"Don't mention it," Marvin mumbled, but smiled nonetheless. "Bye," he said to Loki. He stuck his hands in his pockets and walked back to his car. He kept his gaze down and averted from the family at the door, feeling their eyes on him. He wasn't a smoker, but wished for a cigarette. The dysfunction was like spiders crawling over his skin again.

Ugh, spiders. He recalled the sensation of swallowing them, of breathing them in. He got back in the car, waved to the family, then pulled out.

Maybe it wasn't spiders so much as that peculiar discomfort of a warm shower after being out in the snow for a long time. Not harmful, only a necessary transition period to warmth.

Nonetheless, once back in the car, Marvin grumbled to Colette, "Better?"

"A fantastic start," declared Colette.

Marvin groaned, but with less passion than before. He was distracted recalling the look on Archer's face when he met Loki.

Chapter Fourteen

The pleasant unification of boy and cat was subverted by Marvin's concerns about his next destination. Colette had masterminded the plan for the Mosely family, insisting it was the right thing to do. Yet, the drive allowed Marvin too much time for second-guessing. *Was it enough? Too much?*

As he pulled along the curb near the property, Marvin sighed and put his car into park. "I can't do this over the phone?"

"It'll be so much more rewarding in person," said Colette.

"For you or for me?"

"Oh, Marvin. Just *go*, will you?"

"Fine. Stay here, though." Marvin switched off the engine and unbuckled. "It's weird having you talk in my ear."

"Fine. Just go."

In a huff, Marvin did so, plodding slowly to the door of the property. He looked back toward the car, and Colette waved her hand in a motion that said *go on now, get*. When Marvin hesitated, she shrugged dramatically, pointed to herself, then walked her fingers in his direction and pointed to him. Marvin shook his head and turned to face the door, doubting very much she wouldn't end up following him in one way or another. He knocked, then stared at his feet.

When the door opened, Marvin looked up to see Sara Mosely, baby in her arms. She went white. *Like she'd seen a ghost. The irony.*

Marvin realized that, actually, this was worse. He considered her terrified face, understanding that no ghost that had caused her to react this way. He had.

Instead of feeling powerful, Marvin was flooded with remorse. Archer's mother had responded much the same way, like he was a kind of demon. In the past, it was certain that a visit from Marvin Hoeff himself would have been an unwelcome surprise for anyone. He felt every bit the black rot growing beneath his skin, the terror of the darkness which awaited him if he continued on his current path.

He had to fix it.

This moment of introspection caused him to remain silent longer than was proper and did nothing to set Sara at ease. She shifted from foot to foot as she bounced the baby, eyebrows knitted in concern. "Mr. Hoeff, I'm so sorry. Did I forget you were stopping by? Is it an inspection or something?"

Marvin shook his head, mind still spinning with the way she looked at him. He hadn't realized he had been so awful, and the guilt only further complicated the thought to word pipeline.

"Then, I'm sorry, how can I help you?"

Better to get it out. "Mrs. Mosely, it's come to my attention . . ." He sighed, then rubbed his temples. "I need to tell you . . . This is really important—*argghh.*"

The lines on her forehead creased deeply. "Mr. Hoeff, please just tell me."

"You can't live here anymore," he blurted out.

She jumped as if she'd been hit.

"No, no, I don't mean that," he said, holding his hands out in a panic. Trying to soften the blow, he added, "It's good, okay, I promise."

Her expression was mingled devastation and confusion, and Marvin knew he should have practiced this. A little voice came to his ear which made him stand straight at attention.

"I have a different place that will fit your family better," whispered Colette.

Marvin gulped and nodded, looking into the pale face of Sara Mosely. She appeared no less confused, nor less concerned. "I have a different place that will fit your family better," he repeated.

Sara frowned. "What do you mean?"

"It's a few blocks over, but it has three bedrooms and a backyard." Marvin persisted in spite of Sara's wrinkled brow, listening to Colette's instruction in his ear for guidance. "The catch is, it needs a little work. But if you guys are willing to clean and paint a little, it's yours. If you can do that, I'll knock off $500 a month. So your rent will be less than this place."

Her eyes grew round, and she broke the rhythm of bouncing the baby, who fussed at the cessation. "Are you serious?"

He nodded solemnly as though asked to confirm the death of a loved one. To say the place needed work was a tremendous overstatement. A little spackling, touch-up paint, and a thorough cleaning would render it good as new, and a considerable upgrade from the Grove Street house.

She then leaned against the door frame, cradling the baby in her other arm. "Is there a catch?"

Marvin shook his head. "No. No catch. The work isn't extensive. I—I need the help."

Still, her slight grimace read as uncertainty. She had every reason to be suspicious. Marvin *was* lying, after all: he didn't really need the help. It just seemed a more believable offer. Colette had to know this could be a mistake.

What if this backfires somehow?

"It's okay. Just keep going," said Colette.

Marvin ran his fingers through his hair, deciding that, in this case, being as honest as possible was the best policy. "I'm a jerk," he spat out. "Okay? I know it. Yeah, the place needs some work, but it could easily rent for twice this price. I'm . . . trying to change."

"Good job," Colette whispered. Marvin swatted in her direction, then gulped.

"You've been great tenants. I could use the help." He then shrugged again, as though this favor was of no great importance to him. "And I suspect your family could use the space."

She paused. As her suspicion abated, he remembered why he was doing this. She wasn't looking at him with such fear and revulsion as before. There was a relaxed openness to her expression.

"You're not a jerk," she said with the suppressed smile of a white lie.

Marvin bobbed his head side to side, thinking of her family's gold-laden souls and his own swampy filth which he hoped the deal might loosen.

She continued, "But are you serious? About the three bedrooms and stuff?"

Marvin nodded gravely. "Yup. I mean, if you're not interested that's fine—"

"No, no. *No*," she asserted. "I'm—we're very interested. I'm just . . ." She looked askance, then back to him. "Surprised."

"Yeah. I bet." He raised his hands and let them drop to his side. "Well, anyway, let me know when's good for you and you can check it out." He turned and headed to the car.

"Mr. Hoeff," called Sara. "Marvin."

He turned around.

Sara's lips were parted slightly in a look of mystified joy as she attempted to assemble her thoughts. When she spoke again, it was softly, as though worried that by speaking too loudly she would chase the blessing away. "Thank you."

Marvin shrugged. "It's the right thing," he said, robotically, having hardly said the phrase before in his life.

Mrs. Mosely smiled, apparently having the good sense to stay quiet lest her gift horse get spooked.

When Marvin got into his car, he rubbed his face as though to rid himself of the schmaltz of the moment.

"Good job, Marvin," said Colette, materializing into the seat beside him.

Marvin nodded, a confluence of feelings within him. "Where to next?"

Chapter Fifteen

Colette and Marvin hatched their plan for the next phase of reform over a late lunch from the gas station. It wasn't much, but Marvin was at least grateful it wasn't rotten food served by the corpse-chef.

The sun was up, bright and cheerful, on Marvin's route to the Riverbrook apartments. It was as though Colette's shiny personality had invaded every inch of the world around him. He hesitated each time he had to look in the rearview mirror, not wanting to meet Colette's eyes in case she made herself visible. He hadn't yet figured out any kind of pattern to her visibility or invisibility but was sure it would someday make sense to him.

He entered the apartment complex, pulling beside Abhi's Mazda, then put his car into park. Sighing, he allowed his head to settle against the headrest. It was only mid-afternoon and Marvin felt like he had worked a full week, but making things right with Abhi couldn't wait. And so, he began his walk of shame to Abhi's front door.

Before he could stop himself, he raised his hand and knocked on the door. Footsteps could be heard inside. When Abhi answered, his look of curiosity changed as his thick brow furrowed in derision.

"Mister Hoeff," he said with distinct displeasure.

Marvin felt a nudge at his back, Colette's obvious way of saying, *Go on, tell him you're sorry.* Marvin jumped, causing a slight raise of one of Abhi's brows.

He coughed to cover it, then spoke. "I'm sorry, Abhi."

"Mr. Hoeff?"

Marvin held up a hand to silence him. What he had to say would be difficult enough without interruption. "Please."

Abhi closed his mouth and nodded.

Marvin continued, speaking more quickly than usual. *Best to spit it out*, he supposed. "I was upset yesterday. I said some things I didn't mean and I want to make it right."

Abhi's whole posture changed, his eyes softening. "Sir, thank you for saying this. There was much to take in, of course."

"It's not just yesterday, though." He remembered the plan Colette had insisted upon and closed his eyes for a brief, steadying moment before speaking them. "You're a good manager. A good man. I respect you. And I hope you know that."

Abhi frowned with the same suspicion Marvin had seen in the two women previously, but said, "Thank you, sir."

"Of course," said Marvin, biting the inside of his cheek against the pain of this sentimental conversation. "And whatever it costs, we'll fix up Miss Finch's old unit, good as new. And we will forgive the remainder of the lease, of course." He sighed. "And we will send a gift basket to her father."

Abhi looked flummoxed. "Sir, forgive me, but . . ."

"You also deserve a raise. Is 30% enough?"

"*Sir.*"

"What?"

He lowered his voice. "Is it cancer, sir? Are you all right?"

"Oh, No. Nothing like that." He paused, shaking his head. "Just a change of heart."

Abhi looked hardly mollified by that answer, his eyes searching Marvin for some further explanation.

Marvin ignored the silent barrage of questions and asked his own, "Can I trust you to make sure that happens?"

Abhi paused, puzzled, then finally dipped his chin in assent. "Yes. Yes, sir. It is the least I can do."

"Thank you, Abhi. You do good work." It sounded like a confession more than a compliment.

Nonetheless, it seemed to touch Abhi. There was a warmth to his expression, but it still didn't mask the confusion. "If I may ask?"

Marvin braced himself.

"To what do I owe this change of heart?"

Marvin grimaced in his attempt to smile. "Suppose I had some time to think last night. Something, ahh, got to me, I guess."

Abhi smiled. "Whatever it is, sir, I'm grateful to see it."

"Well, okay, Abhi. That's great." Marvin ran a hand through his hair. "Great. So yeah. You get on that gift basket." He gritted his teeth against the urge to add *but don't spend too much*. He jerked a thumb behind him to indicate he would be leaving. "Meanwhile, I'll go ahead and get the cleanup underway."

Abhi leaned into a moderate bow. "Thank you, Mr. Hoeff. This was far more than I myself could bear. I thank you for taking it upon yourself, sir."

"Don't mention it, Abhi." More threat than assurance, despite Marvin's best intentions.

Still, as he walked away, he reflected on the changes in Abhi's demeanor, the way he looked at Marvin with gratitude, with respect.

It was no longer the reverent fear of approaching a bomb, but something else. The fear-respect had felt powerful. And yet, seeing Abhi melt before him at his apology, at his assurance he wasn't alone in the managing Colette's death scene softened Marvin's heart, too.

He had to admit this new form of respect wasn't so bad.

Chapter Sixteen

Marvin's apology to Abhi, his deal with the Moselys, and the gifting of Loki the kitten represented the beginning of the rest of Marvin's life.

In addition to the gift basket Abhi sent to Colette's father, Marvin sent condolences of his own. They had been delivered in the form of a rather generic card from Hallmark's bereavement section. Still, Colette thought it resembled *real progress*, or so she said as Marvin somewhat reluctantly licked the envelope.

In the weeks that followed, Colette convinced him to stop capricious rent increases. She would allow him to do so only when reasonable, which was—to say the least—far less frequently than Marvin would have preferred. She also negotiated a wage increase for his workers and helped him find better benefits for them.

He thought such things would bankrupt him. Instead, he found he had less turnover of both staff and tenants, and genuinely liked the people he worked with—especially Abhi, who he found less repulsively self-righteous than before. They developed a friendship, one in which Abhi actually did grow respect him, not just treat him with respect.

For the rest of Marvin's life, he developed a name for himself quite unlike his previous reputation. His name was now synonymous with kindness and benevolence, albeit the quiet kind which most attributed to modesty. None understood the secret to why he had turned around, thinking, like the associates of Ebenezer Scrooge, it had simply been a miracle.

Who would imagine anything different?

None would guess that behind all this benevolence was a ghostly Colette. While these actions brought him some semblance of pleasure, the greater impetus was the guardian demon who would scare the shit out of him if he refused.

If he refused to donate regularly to good causes—even the random occasions when Colette insisted he pay for the groceries of a frazzled mother in the supermarket.

If he refused to rent his apartments slightly below market value, and give people a month off when they most needed it.

If he didn't ensure the units were kept to the standard he, himself, would expect to live.

Marvin found himself doing previously unthinkable things, like looking the other way on more than one undocumented pet, even leaving behind bags of pet food now and again (anonymously, of course.) He did persuade Colette to allow him to contribute a not-so-subtle bottle of pet stain cleaner as well.

Occasionally, and far more often than he'd ever admit to, he could be found kicking a ball around with the children in his buildings.

During Christmastime, Colette would assemble a list of families who could use a Secret Santa. She even did a little digging to figure out what to buy for the kids. These families never knew Marvin was behind it but appreciated the Christmas miracles all the same.

Though the stymied growth of his bank account caused physical pain at times, it was nothing compared to what would happen if he refused.

That's not to say Colette made him go broke. Indeed, because of her reconnaissance work, she knew exactly who deserved a break and who didn't. Some prospective tenants would inexplicably turn around when they came for a tour. Others would flee their unit, and Marvin never bothered to ask why. He knew why—and found a certain *schadenfreude* in knowing they had received a well-deserved taste of Colette's dark side, too.

At the end of Marvin's life, Colette was there to welcome him to the other side. He had fallen down the stairs after a heart attack. As he lay there, Colette kneeled beside him and took his hand. It was their first physical contact since the reformation chambers, and Marvin knew exactly what it meant.

It was a bittersweet moment, for, though he didn't want to admit it, Colette had become his best friend.

"I have one last thing to show you," said Colette. She whisked him away to a chapel full of people. Centered at the front was a casket.

Marvin's casket.

It was his funeral.

Marvin looked on slack-jawed.

"Don't you see what you've done?" asked Colette. "Look."

Marvin did. He had never spent much time imagining his own funeral, to be fair. Still, gun to his head, he could hardly have believed many would attend. Even fewer would grieve. Instead, he saw a chapel full of those who had fond memories of him. They were grateful to him. Many spoke of being inspired by his selflessness to be more selfless in their own lives. Archer, now a young adult, was in attendence, as were the Moselys, and even Abhi and his family.

"You left a lot of good things behind," said Colette.

"I guess I did," said Marvin.

"I won't even take credit for it. I'm just happy it happened."

Marvin shot her a look but couldn't help smiling. He looked on at all these people who would miss him now that he was gone. He wouldn't fade into darkness after all. Though he had done his good deeds with a less-than-wholly charitable spirit at first, through the years he found he enjoyed performing them. He found an intrinsic yearning for the warmth which came from performing these acts.

He had done a good thing—many of them—and was now reaping the rewards. His soul wasn't so black as he had seen it once upon a time, and it was all thanks to one person, without whom none of it would have been possible. Pain may indeed tend to beget pain, but in the instance of Marvin and Colette, it had birthed something new.

His eyes misted as he looked at her. "Thank you, Colette."

Colette smiled. "Anytime."

THIS BOOK COULDN'T HAVE been written without many years of renting from less-than-stellar landlords, whom I will thank first. I wrote my first draft of The Tenant while pissed off at our landlord, a man rumored to have sued a dead tenant's family for the remainder of her lease payments. The rumor seemed outlandish when I first heard it. Yet when I met this man in person for the first time, it seemed to fit. He will here remain nameless as, again, this is a work of fiction.

In one rage-fueled week, I sublimated my rage into the book you now hold. It was wonderfully cathartic, but draining. When I finished, I practically chucked the draft at my wonderful developmental editor, Kelly. The writing was so raw I figured it was either be fantastic or terrible. Kelly saw the vision and helped me clarify the story, the setting, and the characters of Marvin and Colette in general. Though the book was written in the spirit of revenge, I wanted more. I wanted to tell a story that had seeds of truth and hope in it… while keeping the deliciously dark suffering of Marvin.

We live in a scary, dark, and fallen world. Despite that, I still believe most people are good at heart—or at least want to be. Maybe it's just something I have to believe to feel any of this is worth it.

I must also thank my friends and family who have watched my children while I edited this book, as well as those who listened to me vent during difficult parts and have actually bought my past book. I couldn't do it without your help—you know who you are.

And thank you, dear reader, for taking a chance on this independently published author. It's tough out here, and your support makes everything possible.

Reviews are the lifeblood of self-published authors, granting our books a chance in a competitive market. If you enjoyed this book—or even if you didn't—I would be immensely grateful if you could take a moment and leave a review of it on Amazon. Your feedback, whether full of praise of criticism, helps readers find the right book.

Thank you wholeheartedly for supporting independent authors.

Odella Howe is a former ghostwriter and married mother of four who is finally fulfilling her dream of being a horror author. Now taking "ghostwriting" literally, she delights in crafting supernatural stories that both terrify and thrill her readership.

From the time she could check out books like *Scary Stories To Read In The Dark*, she loved terrifying tales, and soon moved on to reading such authors as Stephen King and Shirley Jackson.

Her highly rated debut novel The Violin was published in January 2025.

When not writing, Odella enjoys hiking the stunning foothills of Utah, sewing, and spending time with her family.

The Violin

In 1871, Elise Knight makes a deal with the devil: craft a powerful violin in exchange for her fiancé's resurrection. But when her father falls deathly ill before the instrument is finished, Elise must choose between honoring his final wish—or trusting the man who promises her power over the grave.

Available now wherever books are sold.

Orbweaver

Eight-year-old Bella loves her mom, her aunts, and bugs of every kind. She doesn't like her new stepdad—and soon learns she's right not to. As he reveals his true nature, the spider in Bella's room reveals its own.

Coming Late 2026

www.ingramcontent.com/pod-product-compliance
Lightning Source LLC
LaVergne TN
LVHW040103080526
838202LV00045B/3759